I0666815

Dangerous Sanctuary

By J. Q. Rose

Amazon Print ISBN 978-0-2286-0929-2

BWL Publishing Inc.

Books we love to write ...
Authors around the world.

http://bwlpublishing.ca

Copyright 2nd Ed. J.Q. Rose 2019
Orig. Ed. 2016 J. Q. Rose
Cover art by Michelle Lee

Copyright Permission

Permission to use the words to the song *You are My All in All* by Dennis Jernigan attributed to Dennis Jernigan, Shepherd's Heart Music, 7804 Fern Mountain Road, Muskogee, OK 74401

Dedication

To my grandmother Maw, my first reader.

Chapter One

"Wilma, quick! Shut the door! We don't want her escaping from the bedroom." Pastor Christine Hobbs whispered. She pressed her fingers to her lips, signaling Wilma to keep quiet while she surveyed the spacious room.

The bent old lady slammed the wooden door shut with a force that almost knocked it off its hinges. The fugitive was certainly aware of their presence now. The pastor shrugged her shoulders.

"I'm going to check under the bed." Pastor Christine heard the faint ringing of the cell phone in her bag in the living room; however, she was in no position to answer it now. She pulled up the heavy dust ruffle and shined the flashlight under the antique four-poster bed while Wilma wielded the straw broom and waited.

Christine tucked a strand of dark brown hair behind her ear and dived under the bed. As she inched her way along the hardwood floor, dust bunnies and dried bits of food and dirt clung to her black suit coat and slacks. She headed in the direction of the low growling sound.

She had confronted many circumstances not formally taught to young seminarians with stars in their eyes. Today was a prime example. She dared anyone to find a chapter in the textbook detailing guidelines for catching a cat. In the past five years in the pulpit business, she'd faced many realities requiring quick thinking and creativity, and the thirty-two-year-old pastor knew there would be many more in the future.

Christine had promised dear Mrs. Whitcomb she'd find a home for her pet cat, Bitsy, when Mrs. W. went home to be with the Lord. Now she was delivering on her promise, maybe, if she could just catch the dang cat! She and Mrs. Whitcomb's frail sister, Wilma, had chased the speedy creature through several rooms in the old Victorian house, but the nimble black and gray striped cat continued to evade the two women.

This time, she knew she had Bitsy cornered under the bed and hoped she could depend on her partner in the chase to brandish the broom to keep the feisty feline from darting out and away again. What was she thinking? The speed of the old woman could never match the agility of this swift cat.

When the flashlight beamed across the cat's glowing eyes, a cold chill ran down Christine's back. Those eyes were terrifying.

"Okay, Bitsy." She talked softly to the frightened animal. "Please come to me. I'm going to take you home and find someone to take care of you and love you." The growling was much louder. The hairs on the back of Christine's neck stood on end. Would this usually docile cat turn into a tiger and scratch her eyes out? Taking a deep breath, Christine slowly inched forward and offered Bitsy her fingers so she could sniff her hand. "That's a good kitty. You know me from all the times I visited your mistress, don't you?"

Quick as a flash of lightning, Christine grabbed the surprised pet behind her neck and hung on. Growls turned into yowling as she scrambled out from under the bed, dragging the struggling cat, dirt, and dust bunnies with her. She clutched the cat in her arms and scooted back to sit on the floor with her back against the wall, speaking quietly and petting the cat's soft fur to soothe her. After the fierce feline calmed, Christine stood up next to the bed hugging Bitsy to her chest.

"Oh, my. Oh, my," was all Wilma could say when she saw the cat safely in Christine's arms. She unclenched the straw broom and propped it against the wall, then shuffled over to pat the cat's head. "You'll be okay, Bitsy, with Pastor Christine. She'll take good care of you."

"Oh, yes, I will, but only till I can find Bitsy a nice home like I told your sister." Christine smiled at the sweet lady. She freed one hand to brush off the dirt and dust, and now cat hair, on her suit but stopped when Bitsy began struggling to get down.

Christine hurried to retrieve the cat carrier by the kitchen door. Before the cat had a chance to jump away to hide again, she gently shoved the cat into the carrier and latched the door. The yowling cat's protest turned into guttural growls as she settled into the corner of the cage, tail lashing wildly.

"Thanks for your help, Wilma." She stood and faced the eighty-year-old woman who was not exactly adept at catching kitties. Still, she'd offered a lot of moral support.

"Oh, you're welcome. I'll miss her company, but I'm glad to know you'll take good care of her." Wilma's voice choked. "I miss my sister so much. Now I'm all alone."

Christine put her arms around the weeping woman's shoulders and waited for Wilma to compose herself.

"We spent many years together in this house." She pulled a delicate linen handkerchief out of her apron pocket and dabbed her eyes.

Everything would change now for Wilma. She had lost her sister, her pet, her home. She was moving into an assisted living facility at the end of the week. Tomorrow folks from the church would begin packing up everything Wilma wanted to take with her. The remainder of her possessions collected over the sisters' lifetimes would be boxed and donated to the Goodwill. The members volunteered to move her to the facility because there was no family to help Wilma, only the church family. She was counting on all of them to help her settle into her new surroundings.

The pastor hugged the frail woman. "Yes, we'll all miss her." Christine picked up the cat carrier. "Are you okay, Wilma? I can stay with you awhile if you'd like." Christine searched the woman's sad face.

"I'm fine. I'll just get busy packing up a few more boxes. So much to do." Her arms fell to her sides. "You go ahead. I know you have plenty to do too." Wilma smiled and waved her hands to shoo Christine away. "I'm fine."

"Well, I suppose I'd better get Miss Bitsy back to my house and get her situated. I loaded her litter box, bowl, and food in my car. Thanks again for helping me. I'll see you later." She touched Wilma's shoulder. "You get some rest now. God bless you."

* * *

Christine settled the cat in her carrier in the back of her SUV. Bitsy didn't seem so upset now. Hopefully she liked to ride in a car.

She took off for home to drop off the cat and then get back to the church. Having her home in the parsonage across the street from the church was both a blessing and a curse. Close to work, but also available 24 hours a day.

As she approached the house, Christine spotted a police car and ambulance in the church parking lot. She yanked the vehicle's steering wheel so sharply the cat carrier sailed across the back of the car. Her mind raced. *What could be the emergency?* Not taking time to check on the cat, she dashed from her car and sprinted up the steps of the old brown brick church two at a time and raced to the office.

"Oh, Christine. I was just trying to call you again," her secretary, Ella, said.

Christine's face darkened in concern. "Well. I'm glad to see you're okay. What's happened?"

Ella replaced the receiver on the hook. "Dutch found William in the basement. He must have fallen down the steps. We called 9-1-1."

Christine breathed a quick prayer as she rushed down the passing those who had gathered to watch. Ella followed, but it was impossible for her secretary to keep up with Christine's long strides. As she approached the doorway leading to the church basement, a police officer held his palm out to prevent Christine from going downstairs.

"Stop there, ma'am."

"I'm the pastor of this church. I need to see William, our music director. I understand he fell down these stairs." Standing taller, she glared at the officer, challenging him to let her pass.

"I'm sorry, Pastor. No one is allowed down there." He held out his hands to stop her. She tried to discover a way past the officer, but his round body completely blocked the doorway.

She heard Ella and the chorus of church members loudly insist the officer allow the pastor to be with William.

"What's going on up there, Mike?" A gruff voice from the basement yelled up the stairs.

"The pastor wants to come down there, Sir. She is adamant she needs to be with the fallen man."

"Send her down."

"Ella would you please get the cat carrier

and Bitsy's things from my car and see that she's settled in the parsonage." Christine spoke to her secretary before turning back to the police officer, who shrugged and stepped aside to let her pass. She bounded down the wooden stairs, made the turn on the platform, then gasped as she glimpsed the contorted body of the music director at the bottom of the steps. Her stomach lurched when she saw dried blood from a head wound caked on the floor. She grabbed the railing to steady herself while shifting her gaze away from the nauseating scene. She breathed deeply before looking up again.

Two EMTs stood by doing nothing. Her face flushed with a flash of anger but she guessed there was nothing they could do for a dead man.

The medical examiner investigator motioned her to stop on the flight of stairs. "Sorry, ma'am. Don't come any farther. This is a crime scene. This man is dead."

Chapter Two

Christine's stomach turned over as she grasped the railing once more. Her mind couldn't absorb the reality of William lying dead on the floor of the church basement. *No, he can't be dead!* Her world stopped turning at its usual pace. Instead, everything moved in slow motion as the investigator walked up the basement stairs to meet Christine and escort her up the steps.

"Are you alright?" He helped her turn around on the stairs to return to the hallway, holding her arm as she negotiated the steps. Usually she bounced up these steps, but now she felt like she was trying to climb a mountain.

"I'm okay. I, I need to tell the people waiting in the hallway." She stopped before they got to the platform and faced him. "What happened?"

"I won't know until we investigate the scene and I don't want to speculate. All we know is your music director is definitely dead. I'm sorry." His sad eyes revealed his true feelings while he maintained a professional persona.

"It's my job to tell your folks. I'll do it, but you stay with me, okay?"

"I'm fine. I can do it." She pulled back her shoulders and stood taller.

"Well, ma'am, I know you can do it, but it's my job. They'll need you when I leave, that's for sure."

Christine nodded. They would need her and she would need them to find comfort now and later when trying to deal with the loss of their beloved William.

The group moved to the doorway when Christine and the investigator entered the hallway from the basement.

"I'm so sorry, Pastor, folks. There's nothing you can do for Mr. White now, he's gone and the best you can do is go on home. The police are investigating. The area is sealed off and they'll take care of things. Please, go on home." He held his hands up then dropped them to his side. The graying investigator watched as the group stood silently, waiting until they absorbed the news. Gasps of disbelief rose from the crowd. Some began to cry and hug each other, while a few looked too stunned by the news to react.

Christine clasped her hands tightly together in front of her and took a deep breath to give herself strength her before addressing the gathering of onlookers. "I know it's difficult for us to learn William has passed away. We all have questions, but we need to let the police continue their investigation." Christine's heart shattered as she watched the faces of the members of the congregation distorted by anguish and grief. "Let's meet in the chapel in a few minutes."

She turned to Joanie, the Christian Education Director. "Please go with the group to the chapel and lead them in prayers. I'll join you when I can."

Joanie nodded and invited the bystanders to follow her to the chapel area.

Christine sought a chair in the hallway before her knees buckled. Folding her hands in her lap, she asked God for strength to get through these next few moments. William White, their music director and her friend was dead. Cold reality stabbed her heart. She tried to contain the pain and nausea building in the pit of her stomach by folding her arms and holding them tight to her body.

What caused William to fall down that flight of stairs and die on the concrete floor of the furnace room? Tears streamed down her face. She had no answers, but she was determined to find out for the sake of his family and her congregation.

* * *

Christine sat next to Dutch, the church's part-time custodian. His giant-sized body dwarfed the folding chair he sat in. He held his face in his large hands and rocked his body back and forth. A white wadded up handkerchief, wet with his tears, lay in his lap.

She rested her hand on his shoulder to let

him know of her presence. Detective Cole Stephens sat across from them in the small classroom just across the hall from the large sanctuary. He was part of the team investigating William's death.

"Mr. Van Laan, what time did you discover Mr. White?"

"He's already told the other policemen who were here. Does he have to go through this again? He needs to go home."

"Pastor, I need his story while it's still fresh in his mind. I don't want him to forget the details." He fixed his gaze on Dutch. "When did you find the body, Mr. Van Laan?"

Dutch picked up the handkerchief and wiped his eyes, then loudly blew his nose and looked down at his worn boots. "I came in the church about eight this mornin' and began cleanin' the upstairs bathrooms and pickin' up this and that. I went downstairs to get toilet paper off the storage shelf in the furnace room. I turned on the light at the top of the stairway, and when I turned the corner on the platform halfway down the stairwell, I saw...." Dutch wiped his eyes again and took a deep breath. "I saw William layin' on the floor. I ran down the steps, and there he was all crooked and bloody."

"Did you touch the body?"

"Yes, er no....uh." Dutch's eyes darted to the detective and then to Christine.

She squeezed his shoulder, wondering why the detective wasn't making notes in the notebook in his hand. Why keep questioning

Dutch if he wasn't recording the answers? Anger began to build.

Detective Stephens leaned forward in his chair. "Well, what is it? Did you touch him?"

"I'm not sure."

"What do you mean you're not sure? Either you did or didn't." He raised his voice.

"I may have shook him to wake him up." The custodian looked up at Stephens. "I can't remember. I don't know. I can't...I can't..."

"Stop, please. He can't take anymore. You'll have to talk to him later. I'm taking him home now." Christine's eyes blazed as she faced the detective.

She stood up. He looked at her with a smug smile. "Yeah, go ahead and take him home, but you may want to clean up a bit, Pastor. By the way, how did you get that dirty?" His brown eyes twinkled as he scanned her from head to toe.

She looked at the front of her jacket and pants and remembered the dust and food particles still clinging to her clothes. She ignored the detective and went to Dutch. "Come on, Dutch. I'll take you home."

Detective Stephens stood up but did nothing to stop them from leaving.

He called after her, "I'll be back to interview you and the secretary and anyone who was here this morning when the body was found."

Chapter Three

Thank goodness for garage door openers.
Christine cut the SUV into the driveway of the
parsonage as she noted the news media gathered
in the church parking lot. She hit the accelerator
and escaped into the garage the minute the door
opened.

She rested her forehead on the wheel while
the door closed behind her and allowed the
silence to engulf her before facing the chaos.
She just wanted the long day to end. William's
death, Dutch coping with the questions from the
police, counseling his family, upset parishioners
calling.

Christine grabbed her bag and briefcase off
the passenger side floor, and made her way
through the garage. When she opened the door
leading into the kitchen, a dark shadow
disappeared into the dining room. She jumped at
the quick movement and then smiled when she
realized it had to be Bitsy.

"Here, Bitsy. Here, kitty."

Walking into the house owned by the
church and maintained by the parsonage
committee was like re-visiting the '70's era. The
interior of the house was decorated, if that's
what you'd call it, in avocado green and harvest
gold. The harvest gold kitchen appliances
functioned well thanks to regular maintenance

by a church member who was a retired electrician.

Christine dropped her bag and keys on the kitchen counter and called the frightened cat. From the presence of the full bowls of water and food on the kitchen floor, she knew Ella had taken care of Bitsy. Even the litter box was filled and ready. She imagined her kind secretary stayed awhile and comforted Bitsy, too.

"Here, kitty, kitty, kitty. Here, Bitsy."

The doorbell buzzed. She wanted to ignore the clamoring reporters outside on the front porch but knew they would only hound her until she talked to them. Opening the door to a sea of cameras and people shouting questions, she motioned to the group for silence and then announced, "I have no comment at this time." She heard protests and more questions as she shut the steel door, locked it, and slid the security bolt in place.

Setting her briefcase on the floor beside her chair, Christine plopped down in her one recliner in the living room.

Bitsy peeked out from behind the couch. Scooting to the front of the chair, she bent down and motioned to the cat. "Come on, kitty. Come on over here, Bitsy."

The cat warily approached. "Here, kitty, kitty, kitty." Just as she sat back in the recliner, the cat leapt onto her lap. Christine ran her hand from the top of the cat's head, along her spine, all the way across the fluffy tail. Bitsy arched her back and purred. Kneading her front paws into Christine's legs, her purring grew louder and louder.

As Bitsy settled on her lap, Christine loosened her tight muscles and gazed around her sparsely furnished living room. The neutral landlord-white wall color a sterile background for the heavy green and gold draperies at the picture windows in the front of the house.

But she felt at home with the over-sized lamp on the end table near the recliner, a few folding chairs from the church, and an old couch which fit right into the parsonage's '70's décor. A gray card table and chairs served as a temporary dining table in the dining room just off the kitchen and living room.

Her bedroom upstairs contained the handsome dark cherry bedroom suite, remnants of her marriage to Brad. They were the only items she had fought for after their divorce two years ago.

She smiled as she looked into the cat's face and continued petting its smooth, silky coat. In a sense, assuming the care of this pet would be one of her more pleasant duties as church pastor. This career took most of her time. Even after nine months, she hadn't made time to furnish her home. Instead, she'd concentrated on being the spiritual leader of the three hundred souls at Dayspring Church in Fair Lake, Michigan.

Christine closed her eyes for a minute and then quickly opened them to dispel the vision of

William sprawled on the basement floor. How would she ever erase that image from her mind? She rubbed her eyes in an attempt to ward off a dull headache forming behind her eyes.

Her thoughts turned to Dutch, the sweet man who entertained the Sunday School kids, helped out with church dinners, and took pride in making the church shine. After the detective interviewed him in the Sunday school room, Christine spent several hours with the distraught man and his family at their home. His wife, Kendra, and their two grown children were outraged that the police suspected their husband and father of murder.

In her mind, Christine began to construct the words she would need to notify William's sister of his death. Even with her years of experience behind her, it was never easy to tell a family member or friend their loved one was dead.

Hi sister Claire lived an hour away, and Christine hoped she hadn't already heard about his accident on the news. As far as she knew Claire and her husband were William's only family. He had never talked about an ex-wife or a girlfriend. Christine's brow crinkled when she considered that after nine months of working with William at the church, she really didn't know much about him, as he'd never spoken about his personal life.

She grinned when she remembered his tousled thick brown hair, warm eyes, and deep laughter echoing throughout the church hallways. Christine pictured him dressed in one of his famous T-shirts. He had a reputation for his T-shirt collection. Every time she saw him, he wore a different colorful shirt graced with clever, humorous sayings and graphics.

Christine and William shared a love of music. For the thirteen years of his tenure as music director at Dayspring Church he'd proven himself an accomplished musician. His performances on the organ filled the hearts of the congregation with awe and wonder and as choir director he'd taught the choir members to mesh their voices beautifully and bring the presence of God into the sanctuary.

He considered the members of the children's choir "his" kids, and shared their excitement whether they were playing a sport, performing in a play, or winning a science award. He'd been well known and loved in the community from his participation in service groups outside of the church. Christine's eyes teared up. She would miss him and his lively spirit.

Christine jumped when the doorbell buzzed, followed by a loud, "Yoo-hoo!" The cat hopped off her lap, and Christine climbed out of the recliner. She rushed to unlock and open the kitchen door. Lacey marched in with a bouquet of flowers and a brown paper bag.

"Hey, Chris. How ya' doin'?" Lacey placed the vase of red and yellow tulips on the kitchen counter and walked toward Christine. "I heard about William. I'm so sorry." Lacey wrapped her arms around Christine and hugged hard.

The tall pastor and the petite florist couldn't have been more different in appearance. Lacey's blunt cut strawberry blonde hair and bright floral shirt and jeans contrasted with the minister's black suit and shoulder length brown hair. Because they were so alike in their life experiences, they'd become fast friends. They were nearly the same age, both single, both uncommitted, and both had marriages that had ended badly.

Lacey held out the brown bag. "Here, I brought us some light beers. I figured you needed some company." She smiled big, reminding Christine how much she loved her friend.

"You're so thoughtful. Thanks for the beer and the beautiful flowers."

"Aw, you're welcome." Lacey waved off the comment and moved toward Bitsy.

"What a sweet kitty. Is this Mrs. Whitcomb's cat? She's beautiful." Lacey bent down to pat the now friendly feline.

"Yeah, that's Bitsy. She wasn't interested in coming home with me." Christine watched as her friend easily stroked the cat. "You certainly have a way with cats. It took me quite awhile before Bitsy would even look at me. Have a seat."

Each grabbed a beer and twisted off the caps as they settled themselves on the big ugly couch for a warm heart-to-heart talk. Bitsy chose to stretch out on the back of the couch lounging between the two women. For a few minutes, the pastor relaxed and allowed herself to forget her responsibilities and just enjoyed having a friend. Lacey helped to fill the void Christine had felt after divorcing Brad, whom she thought would be her soul mate forever.

"I heard Cole Stephens is the investigator on William's case," said Lacey. "He's gorgeous." She grinned a silly face at Christine and then sucked down more beer.

"You've got to be kidding me. I was so worried about Dutch, I didn't even notice."

"Well, I'm sure you had your mind on a lot more than Cole Stephens. Take my word for it, he's a cutie." Lacey winked.

Christine tried to picture Cole Stephens. He was a tall, muscular man and handsome in his tie and sport coat. She remembered his short-cropped hair. Was it a flattop, or was there some spiky hair sticking out? Did he wear glasses or not? Her memory of him was too fuzzy.

"I didn't exactly have my man radar out this morning." She tried to brush off more of the cat hair, dust, and food particles on her suit coat and slacks.

"Well, I'm sure he'll be talking to you some more if this investigation turns up foul play."

Christine sat straight up on the couch and faced her friend. "Why would you even say something like that? You know William probably just tripped down the steps. Gosh, Lacey. What a thing to say!"

"I'm just sayin'…just wondering…I mean,

really, Chris, nobody knows anything about William. He may have had too much wine and fell down the steps, or maybe he discovered a burglar in the church, or any of a dozen things. Just sayin'..." Lacey quickly took another swig of the cold beer.

Focusing intently on Christine's eyes, she said, "Cole Stephens has a reputation for digging for the truth. He won't settle for any old explanation of William's death. You have to be prepared for the worst."

Chapter Four

"Thank you for your comforting words, Pastor." Claire White Armstrong gave Christine a hug at the door of the sanctuary after the funeral service.

"You'd think you'd known Willie all your life. Your message was right on about him." Mr. Armstrong pumped Christine's hand. The man's little round glasses bounced on his nose as he shook his head up and down while he talked.

"Thank you, Mrs. Armstrong. I really enjoyed working with William. I admired his work with the choirs, especially the children's choirs, and his talent for playing the organ. Truly a gift from God. And, oh, those colorful T-shirts." Christine smiled.

Mrs. Armstrong laughed lightly. "Oh, yes, those crazy shirts. I always kept my eye out for the perfect one for him." She grabbed Christine's hand between her palms and held on for a minute. "Thank you, Pastor. He was a very special person." Her eyes glistened with tears.

Christine touched her shoulder. It was difficult to speak with the emotion blocking her throat.

"I believe the ladies of the church have the luncheon ready downstairs. Shall we meet with

William's friends? I'm sure they'd love to share the good times they had with William."

As she accompanied the Armstrongs down the main stairwell, Christine felt good about the memorial service, an impressive and loving celebration of his life. The chancel choir, hand bell ensemble, small orchestra, and the children's choirs presented the music he loved so much. She, along with her pastoral duties, played the Bach piece that was William's favorite according to his choir members. She felt comforted by the experience and touched by the tributes presented by the members of the congregation.

The family piece of mixed spring flowers from his sister added vibrant color to the setting. Next to the flowers and the urn containing his ashes, a framed photo of William in one of his signature T-shirts smiled out to the large group of friends attending the celebration of his life.

* * *

Christine left the basement fellowship hall to return to her office after the family and friends departed from the post-funeral luncheon. As she hung her black jacket in its place in the small closet in her office, someone cleared his throat in the doorway. Christine turned to find Cole Stephens leaning on the doorframe, staring at her. She noticed his short haircut, wide shoulders, and handsome face with no glasses. Lacey was right. He was attractive.

"Hello, Detective Stephens. Were you at William's funeral?"

Christine smiled when he stood tall and straightened his conservative black tie. He wore a black suit in deference to the grieving family.

"Yes, I was there. Quite a show."

She closed the closet door and turned back to face him with hands on her hips. "What a thing to say. Not exactly a show, Detective. The members wanted to share their love and the musical talent William White developed through his leadership."

"Oh, yes, and the bigger and better the program, the more money donated to the church coffers." He sat down in the chair across from the desk.

Christine remained standing, clenching her fists to her side. "What brings you here? I didn't realize you knew William that well."

"I figured I'd come and watch."

"What? Watch for what?" Curious now, she sat in her leather desk chair, wondering how such a man was endowed with good looks, but no charm or manners.

"I wanted to see who came to the service. The murderer usually shows up at his victim's funeral."

Chapter Five

"Are you telling me William was murdered? That's ridiculous!" Grasping the top of her desk, Christine leaned forward to confront the detective. "Why would you even say such a thing?"

Stephens tried not to smile at her outrage. He liked the way her blue eyes blazed with fury. "The autopsy is complete. There is no other explanation for his death. No heart attack, stroke, seizure. Even if he tripped down the steps, the evidence doesn't prove it was a simple fall." He picked up a pen teetering on the front edge of the desk and placed it in front of the aggravated pastor. His helpful gesture did not seem to calm her.

"I'm afraid all the members of this congregation, including you, Pastor, and the entire staff, are all persons of interest in this case. I'll need to interview the choir members and musicians and especially those who were here at the church on that Wednesday evening." He stood up facing her. "Now please direct your secretary to give me the contact information for those people. I'd appreciate your cooperation." He could see the minister's wish to choke him in her eyes. *Damn, she's got beautiful eyes.*

She clenched her jaw and sat taller to

maintain a professional manner. "All right, Detective, I'll have our secretary give you a member directory. It was updated last fall and Ella will know if there are any names to be added to the list. Please follow me down to the office."

Detective Cole trailed behind the shapely preacher, his gaze taking in her long legs as she strode quickly down the hall without glancing back at him. Her shoulder length hair flipped out from her head as she speed-walked to the church office and stepped inside the room.

When Cole caught up to Christine, she was standing at the secretary's cluttered desk.

"Ella." Cole noticed the change in the pastor's voice and body language as she approached the secretary. Ella grabbed a tissue from the box at the corner of her desk and dabbed at her eyes. Christine bent toward her and asked, "Are you okay? Do you need to go home?"

"She can't go home till I get the names of the congregation and staff contacts." He moved into the room. Ella looked at her pastor and then at the detective. She blew her nose.

"Okay, Detective. Wait a minute. Can't you see this has been a difficult day for us here?" The pastor's icy glare bore into him.

Her face softened as she spoke gently to the grieving secretary. "Ella. Detective Stephens is here because he's investigating William's accident."

Cole didn't interrupt. If she wanted to

believe it was an accident instead of murder, so be it. She was protecting herself and probably the secretary from the full force of the idea that anyone in her church could be capable of murder.

"He needs to talk to some of the people who were here Wednesday evening, so he asked for the member directory. We have an extra one here, don't we?"

The detective looked around at the small, crowded office. Piles of papers lay on every counter space available. Filing cabinets, an undersized table, and an oversized copy machine shared the limited floor space with an enormous jumbled up desk and bookshelves not exactly arranged in library-like order. He didn't even want to imagine what lurked behind the doors of the wooden cabinets hanging on the wall.

Ella pushed back her chair and moved to a filing cabinet. She immediately pulled out a thin spiral-bound book for the detective. "You can keep this one. We have a few more." She gently placed the directory into his hand, and her lips curved into a smile.

* * *

In her paneled office, Christine tried to relax at her desk. She kept re-playing the detective's words in her head, "The murderer usually shows up at his victim's funeral." A dull headache settled in her brain.

She picked up the pen Cole had placed on her desk, dropped it back in the drawer and slammed it shut. If only she could shut out the memory of Cole Stephens and his attitude that easily. Something about the man bothered her.

She felt more at ease in the office as she sat in the silent room. After almost nine months as the minister of Dayspring Church, she had made the space her own with photos of her smiling parents, her beloved brothers' families, and school pictures of her nieces and nephews. Favorite wall hangings she had brought back home from mission projects in Costa Rica and special mementoes of her ministry added coziness to the room.

She caressed the little gifts from friends, a wooden box from Haiti, the handmade cards from the women in Zimbabwe, an olivewood camel statue from the Holy Land. Her laptop sat on the cherry wood desk among research books and newspapers, cherished Bibles, and commentaries. They were all reminders of her reason to be here, in this place, at this time.

She was not going to allow this horrible event to ruin her church and the lives of her church family. She counted many of the nearly three hundred parishioners as friends and loved them for their Christian hearts and actions. *Help us, Lord. Be with us. Hold us in the light of your love. We need your comfort and peace throughout this ordeal. Help me to lead my parishioners and find the words I need to move us forward and stay strong.*

Christine opened her eyes and breathed deeply. She tried to forget Cole Stephens' suspecting a member of her congregation of murder. He was so sure of himself. But what if he was right?

How did William die? Why would someone want to kill him?

Chapter Six

The next morning the cell phone blasted Beethoven's "Fifth Symphony" through its impressive sounding speaker. Christine jumped from her desk chair and rummaged in her large tote bag to find and answer it. She didn't recognize the phone number but decided to take the call anyway.

"Hobbs, we need a preacher now!" The voice on the phone was firm and left no doubt about the urgency of the situation. "This is Stephens. I'm pulling into the church parking lot. Get out here right away."

Christine locked out her office window to see the black Ford pulling into the parking lot and on its way to the double doors of the church entrance. She grabbed her bag and flew down the steps.

She opened the passenger door and hopped in. "What's going on? You're scaring me to death!"

"Two blocks from here one of your parishioners is being held hostage with a knife at his throat. His hyped-up grandson is using him as a shield to keep the officers away. We've been talking to him since early this morning. He asked for you."

"Who's the hostage?"

"Roger Jenkins. His grandson is Jason Jenkins."

Christine swallowed hard. Roger Jenkins was indeed a church member and had been for fifty years, dearly beloved as one of the saints in the church. She had visited his wife in the nursing home several times.

The morning sun highlighted the new leaves on the trees. The tulips were at their peak of color. This was a day full of beauty and promise. No one would suspect the dark drama taking place at the small white wooden frame house on Pine Street.

Stephens pulled the car along the curb. Christine jumped out and hurried toward the policeman who motioned to her to stay low to the ground. Dread fell over her as she realized the policeman was trying to keep her from being a target if Jason had a gun. He held a cell phone in front of him and was talking to the kid inside the house.

"Okay, Jason. We have your grandfather's pastor here," the officer announced into the phone. He ducked down behind the car and turned to the crouching minister, greeting her with a quick nod.

"Hello, Pastor. Can you help us out here and talk this guy out of the house to give us some time till the negotiator gets here? The kid asked to talk to you. He's threatening to kill his grandfather if we storm the place. We think he's high, probably looking to steal some money from grandpa to buy more drugs."

"Anyone else in there with him and Jason?"

"No, no signs of anyone else in there, just the old man and the boy. Let me give you this to speak to him. Maybe you can talk some sense into him."

Christine slightly rose with the phone pressed to her ear. She used the car to shield most of her body as she looked toward the house.

"Jason, this is Pastor Christine. Can I come in and talk with you?"

"Wait a minute, wait a minute, Pastor. You aren't going in there to talk. You stay right here. A hostage specialist from the state police will be here soon. You just calm the boy down." She ignored the policeman's stern voice and kept her eyes on the doorway of the house.

The strong young man dragged the frail old man to the screen door. Jason kept his arm around his grandfather's neck. The blade of a butcher knife gleamed in his hand. His left arm circled the old man's waist, holding him upright in the doorway.

"I'm tired of talkin'. I don't wanna talk to nobody! Everybody leave, so I can get outta here!" His hoarse voice strained to shout at the surrounding police.

Christine unfolded from her crouched position and moved around the car into full view.

"Jason, let your grandpa go. We can talk. Let me come in. We can work this out." She moved slowly toward the wooden porch. She tried to breathe deeply and remain calm, but her heart thundered in her chest.

Her eyes held the young man's as she tried to talk him down. Suddenly the frail old man collapsed and slipped from his grandson's grasp. Christine raced toward the porch.

"Granddad, Granddad." He caught his grandfather before he hit the wooden floor and gently laid him down on the porch.

In an instant, the police swarmed Jason and dragged him to the ground, leaving Christine flat on the lawn of the front yard. The boy wailed and cried and called for his Grandfather. "Granddad, Granddad. I'm sorry. I'm sorry." Christine stood up on shaky legs and watched the EMTs revive the unconscious man and work to stabilize him.

* * *

Detective Stephens and Christine watched as the policeman shoved the boy in the back seat of the police car.

"May I talk to Jason?"

"Maybe later, Hobbs. We have to book him. I'll call you if he wants to see you," Stephens said.

"I'll go to the hospital. You'll call Mr. Jenkins' daughter, right? Tell her I'll meet her there?"

Stephens nodded. "Yeah, we'll send a policeman over there to escort her to the hospital if she wants to check on her father or go to the jail to visit her son." In a gruff voice, he said, "I'll take you back to the church. Get in the car."

"Yes, thank you." She made her way to the black Ford, distinctly aware Detective Stephens was upset.

In the car, he started up the engine, then turned to Christine. His face was red as a Michigan apple. "Well, that was some dumb thing you did today. Do you realize you jeopardized the old man's life? That kid was so hopped up on drugs we didn't know what he'd do. The boy could've come at you with his knife or even a concealed gun. You don't get what a dangerous position you were in. If you'd gotten hurt or killed, I could've been booted out of the department."

"Oh, so you're upset because I could have lost your job for you? Is that it?" Christine turned away from him and faced forward, glaring through the windshield. She'd used her instincts to try and save the boy and his grandfather, and approaching the house had worked to get him to the door. Of course, she hadn't thought too far ahead to the consequences if it hadn't worked.

Cole jammed the car into gear and streaked onto the roadway.

She refused to look at the detective. "Then why did you even bother to come after me? I thought you wanted me to help calm the boy down and get him away from his grandfather."

Stephens ignored her. Deep silence filled

the car, and only the songs of the birds on this sunny morning broke it during the drive back to the church.

Stephens stopped the car at the side doors of the church. He placed his hand on the door handle and turned to face her. In a controlled and deliberate tone, he said, "Thank you. I put you in danger, and it won't happen again. It was poor judgment on my part."

"Actually, Detective, I'm glad you did come to get me. I acted on an impulse because I didn't want Roger or Jason hurt. I understand and appreciate your concern."

Cole looked away and fidgeted with the steering wheel. "Well, don't ever try anything like that again. Next time no one may be backing you up. Okay?" His voice softened and his brown eyes penetrated her heart.

"Oh, Detective, God willing I won't be in such a situation ever again." She smiled, opened the car door, and swung her lean legs out to stand on the asphalt parking lot pavement. "Thanks for the ride." She slammed the door shut and took the church steps two at a time.

Chapter Seven

Early Sunday morning, Christine sat in the quiet sanctuary of the decades old church. Her church. The one she was charged with to serve God, the congregation, and the community. She breathed in the scent of the polished wood. Master carpenters had trimmed out the church in rich, dark oak. She imagined them working and using their talents in building such a loving tribute to honor their Lord. The congregation were responsible caretakers of the building, which was a landmark in the small community.

She sat near the back, so she could see the entire front of the church in its wide scope. A pot of pink tulips adorned the altar this Sunday morning. The two pulpits were draped in white after the Easter season. The pipe organ and piano flanked the choir seating area. William's absence at these keyboards would be a painful reminder to the church family.

The wooden railing defined the area where the members of the congregation could kneel for communion or prayer. The spring banners, decorated with floral designs, the cross, butterflies, lilies, and sun rays, hung on each side of the altar adding warmth to the setting.

The rising sun beamed through the stained glass windows, coloring the interior of the room with prism-like reflections.

She bowed her head and whispered, "This is the day the Lord has made. Let us rejoice and be glad in it. Dear Creator, what a glorious spring morning. Thank You for this time to be together with my congregation. Please bring peace and healing to them through my words.

"I ask You to be with William's friends and family as they go about their lives adjusting to his absence. Give the police the insight and determination to find William's killer, so he cannot kill anyone else.

"And for me, yes Lord, help me to find a way to prove Dutch and myself innocent of this crime." She hesitated, knowing she had to empty her heart.

"Lord, I have so much to do. I cannot allow a distraction like Cole Stephens into my life. Help me to focus on the work of the church, Your work. My heart isn't healed enough to give it away again to another man." She exhaled.

"Thank you for your blessings. In Jesus' name, Amen."

After talking with God, Christine rose to attend to her Sunday tasks, feeling God's presence and her soul filled with renewed strength and peace.

* * *

After the service, the long line of parishioners waiting to shake hands and greet the pastor snaked back into the sanctuary, but Mrs. Rappaport continued to hold the minister's hand and monopolize the pastor's attention. "You know, I just love your shoes, Pastor Christine. Oh, and my son, Ralph, is coming home next weekend. I'll bring him to church next Sunday, so you can meet him. He's a wonderful man, divorced, like you. Sorry to say he has no children, but he's still young enough, and that could change." She smiled, and her eyes danced.

"I'm sure he likes to return to his home church to see all his old friends. You have a wonderful day now. God bless you." Christine disengaged from the older woman. Standing in the doorway of the sanctuary, she knew there would be more mothers of sons coming through the line telling her how smart, handsome, and available their sons were. Everyone was a matchmaker in this congregation.

* * *

Late Sunday evening the familiar tune on Christine's cell phone played, interrupting her reading. She fumbled with the newspaper, trying to decide whether to fold it or toss it to the floor by her recliner. She tossed it and grabbed her phone from the end table without checking the ID of the caller. "Hello. This is Pastor Christine."

"Hello, Chris." Christine instantly recognized the voice of her ex-husband, Brad. Her stomach flipped. She'd heard nothing from him since she'd moved to take the position as minister of the Dayspring Church.

"Hi. What's up?" She didn't want to make small talk or even talk to him at all. She didn't want to get emotional. He'd broken her heart.

They had a long history together. They met as undergrads at Michigan State. He was in pre-med and she in music. Her roommate's boyfriend fixed them up their sophomore year. When they were together, the sun shone brighter, food tasted better, and kisses were sweeter. Their relationship magically clicked. She had found her partner for life.

"When I cleaned out the apartment, I found some old photos and yearbooks that are yours. What's your address? I can mail them to you." He sounded as detached as if he were making a business call.

Their senior year, he asked her to marry him after graduation. After the wedding, she began teaching and Brad started medical school. After he flunked out his second year of school, he found a job selling pharmaceuticals and became a valued salesman. His work took him away from home for days at a time, but when he returned, he and Christine came together with love and laughter. But somewhere in the next years of marriage, they lost the magic.

"Oh, I thought I gave it to you. Just use the church's address on Adams Street." She tried to sound calm and upbeat.

"Let me see, now. Oh yeah, here it is. But that isn't where you live. Do I have your house address?" He sounded very formal. Christine wondered if there was an ulterior motive for this call. Maybe he wanted to visit her. Maybe he had some papers to serve her. Stop being paranoid, she thought.

"Well, the parsonage is right across the street, so I just use the church address for my mail. I'm there more than at home." She tried to keep the conversation light, but her heart felt heavy.

"So how are you getting along there with your new church position?" His voice moderated. "You may not believe it, but I do think of you and wonder how you are."

Her eyes teared up. He had no idea how much she missed him and hated him at the same time.

"I'm fine. How're you?"

"Well, as soon as I get this apartment cleaned up, I'll be happy. What a job. I never knew moving would be so difficult."

"You're moving? Where are you going?" She bit her lip. She hated to sound as if she were the least bit interested in his life.

"Nadia and I found a house." He delivered it like a hot poker through her heart.

He met Nadia while he was away on a lengthy sales trip. She shook her head to erase the dark thoughts in her mind.

"We decided it was such a good deal, we couldn't pass it up. I'll send you my new address. It's a ranch-style house in a subdivision near that greasy spoon cafe we liked to go to. Do you remember that place? Jake's." His remarks were so off-handed.

"Oh, yeah." Christine remembered Jake's like

it was yesterday.

Jake's was the place where she told Brad she was pregnant with their baby. She remembered the joy in his face and excitement they felt about beginning their family.

She squeezed her eyes closed, trying to blot out the memory of the night she lost her baby girl in the emergency room. She was all by herself because Brad was away on a business trip. He never understood her feeling of loss because when she tried to talk about the baby, he ignored her, acting like it never happened. The baby wasn't real to him, but Christine had carried the baby close to her heart for five months. Christine loved her. The baby's death devastated her.

She realized she wasn't listening to a word he'd spoken, so when Brad stopped talking she said, "Okay. Thanks. Gotta go. Just mail them to the church. Good-bye." The lump in her throat prevented her from continuing the phone conversation.

Still clutching the phone in her hand, the memories of that Saturday morning conversation over two years ago surfaced in her mind. She and Brad were sitting at the kitchen table. Christine looked forward to spending time with her husband. Having a weekend together was unusual.

"So what are your plans for this weekend? Do you want to take a drive or go to a movie?" she asked as she picked up the cereal box.

Setting his coffee mug on the kitchen table, he looked directly into her eyes.

"I won't be here this weekend."

She stopped pouring the sugary flakes of cereal into the bowl. "Oh, really?" She turned to face her beloved husband. "I thought we could do something fun this weekend. We have so little time together anymore."

"I'm moving out today." He sat motionless in the chair.

"What? What did you say?" She leaned in closer toward Brad, the cereal box clenched in her hand.

"I'm leaving. I'm moving in with a friend. I want out of this marriage." He grabbed the cup of coffee and pulled it toward him.

Christine clutched her stomach to stop the churning inside. Was she dreaming? This couldn't be real. She tried to read his face, but he kept his eyes on his coffee mug.

She slammed the box of cereal down on the table and curled her hands into tight fists. With each sentence she spoke, her fists hit the table. "Wait a minute. Bradley, wait a minute. What's happening? What are you saying?"

He glanced up furtively. Finally locking his gaze on her, he said, "I'm in love with another woman. It's over for us." He scooted back the kitchen chair, turned his back to her, and strode to their bedroom.

She clung to the edge of the table as the room swirled around her. Placing a hand to her forehead to stop the dizziness didn't help. She remained at the table, shell-shocked, silent, and helpless.

Blinking back to reality, Christine threw the cell phone on the end table and covered her face with her hands. A torrent of tears puddled in her palms, then trickled down her wrists. Christine heard heartbreaking cries, then realized the sounds came from her, from the depths of her soul. The phone conversation stirred up all the memories and hurt she thought long buried. No matter how hard she tried, forgiveness was too difficult, not to mention forgetting. No man would ever again win her heart, then crush it.

Chapter Eight

Feeling better the next morning, Christine headed toward the kitchen, looking forward to an eye-opening cup of coffee. After a restless night thinking about Brad, their history together, their baby, his betrayal, and her heartache, she was determined to move on. She wanted to forgive Brad and thought she had until his call last night. She shook her head. *I have lots more work to do on forgiveness. With God's help, I can do it and move on.*

"Bitsy!" Christine shooed the tiger cat off the kitchen counter. She sat down at the small table in the eat-in kitchen, looking forward to the sweet bowl of sugar-coated cereal flakes drowned in cold milk.

Sunshine streamed through the windows lending a cheery glow to the room. She appreciated the clean windows and freshly washed curtains, courtesy of the women's church group. Their work helped to brighten the kitchen, not update it, but brighten it.

The cat rubbed against her legs. She mindlessly petted the friendly animal. The purring was a peaceful accompaniment to reading the devotionals for the morning.

"Hey, Bitsy, it's been a week, and you're still here." She couldn't resist picking up the furry pet.

"I may have to put a notice in the newsletter that you're looking for a home with a nice family. I made a promise to Mrs. Whitcomb to find someone special to love and care for you like she did."

The loud buzzing of the front door bell interrupted her peaceful moment. She knew it couldn't be one of the parishioners since they always came to the kitchen door.

When she opened the door, Cole Stephens stood on the porch. He looked better than ever in his navy blue blazer, white shirt, red striped tie, and khaki pants. Her heart skittered as she gazed into his intense brown eyes. Then she remembered her resolve to shield her heart from hurt. Still, a healthy woman like herself had the right to appreciate a handsome male. For just a moment she could allow herself to savour his golden hair and spring sun-bronzed skin.

"Hello, Detective. Do you need me again to help with a hostage situation?"

No smile, no reaction. Just a question. "May I come in?"

"Oh, sure. Come on in. Would you like a cup of coffee?"

"No, ma'am." He stood in the foyer. She felt his eyes on her as she walked toward the kitchen. "This isn't a social call."

She stopped and took a deep breath before turning. "Oh, I'm sorry. How can I help you?"

"You need to get your jacket and purse and come with me to the station. We need to talk to you about the death of William White." He delivered this as if he had rehearsed it.

She tugged a strand of her hair behind her ear. "Well, I've already talked with you and the police about that night. Do I have to go through the whole thing again?"

"Yes, we have some follow-up questions for you. After talking with several more people, we just want to cover everything."

"Really? Like what?" The hairs on her neck rose.

"Believe me, I'm sorry to have to tell you, but things have come to light making you a person of interest in this case."

"Does that mean I'm a suspect? That you believe I could have killed William?" Christine was astounded. "I'm the pastor of this church. How can you even think such a thing?" Incensed by such a ridiculous idea, she stiffened her arms to her sides and clenched her fists. "You can't be serious!" She walked toward the detective.

Cole held his palms wide. Discarding his official detective attitude, he said, "Hey, hold on now. We do need to clarify some things. Please, just get your jacket, and let's go. You can ride with me and the other officer who's at your back door."

She moved to the back window, pulled the ugly drape aside, and scanned the yard. Yes, there was a policeman standing near her back door. Looking over her shoulder, she snapped at Cole. "Did you think I'd run out the back when I saw you coming?" She jerked the drape across the window. "I know exactly where the city police department is and the city jail, too. I don't need a ride." She had visited parishioners and their friends at the jail several times bringing a message of hope and forgiveness. If churches had no sinners, then there would be no need for churches. "I can't go this morning. I have an appointment at ten o'clock."

"We'll let you cancel it from the station if you need to. I don't know how long it'll take, but you need to come with us now."

Christine bristled at being ordered to go with Cole and the officer, but she had nothing to hide. Besides this interview could convince the police she and Dutch were innocent.

* * *

The small town police headquarters only had a few rooms. White paint covered the walls, woodwork, and doors in a bland monotony of absent color. A jumble of desks sat scattered around the room. An alcove for the communications desk sat in one corner, and the smell of stale air clouded the entire space. Although the spring day was balmy, no windows were open to allow the fresh air in.

Detective Stephens ushered her into a small room for the interview. The closeness of the room was stifling. The fluorescent ceiling light glared harshly in the stark room. He pointed to a chair at the end of the table. "Sit here, Pastor."

As she sat, she felt him watching her. Christine didn't scoot the uncomfortable folding chair under the table, preferring room for her long legs. She felt trapped in the small space. Her back was to the door with no other visible exits.

He pulled out the chair at the side of the long table pushed up against the white wall. "Detective Barton is joining us."

A paunchy detective with thinning gray hair and suspenders holding up his baggy pants, took his place at the far end of the table. He scribbled down notes as they talked.

Christine tried to act relaxed and confident, but a colony of butterflies fluttered in her stomach. "I don't understand. Why would you even think I had something to do with this?"

"Pastor Hobbs, we need to ask you a few more questions." Detective Barton looked over the top of his reading glasses, completely ignoring her question.

Stephens began by asking where she was on that night and when she last saw William White alive. She calmly answered the questions. Again.

"Is it true, Pastor that you are an accomplished organist?"

"Yes, I majored in organ at college and have been playing all my life." The question surprised Christine.

"Is it true you and Mr. White disagreed on music chosen for the worship services?" Christine began to answer but Detective Barton interrupted her. "And is it true at the weekly meetings for planning the worship service, you and Mr. White loudly discussed differing ideas?"

"Well, of course we had to exchange different

ideas in order to allow the best possible worship experience for our congregation. We worked together as a team to accomplish that." Christine remembered a few exchanges with William that became heated and loud. He was a perfectionist, and at times, he believed his selection to be the only one to add the most meaning and depth to the service.

"We had some disagreements, and like all adults, we discussed them and came to a compromise on each point." Of course, she didn't mention William wasn't pleased with every single compromise.

"Could you have been so angry and upset with the music director that you wanted to get rid of him? In fact, you did ask another parishioner to be the organist to replace White's duties every Sunday?"

"Well, yes, I did but not behind William's back. It was after he had come to me asking for some reduction in his responsibilities. We thought that would be one way to help him out. He was trying to grow the music program and wanted to attend some classes and study new music." Christine easily defended herself. She remembered the day he came to her asking for some time off and to suggest the name of an organist to substitute for him during his absence.

"Pastor Hobbs." She faced Cole. She noticed the formal address. "Do you have anyone who can verify where you were on the evening William White was murdered?"

"Well, I was at the church for the weekly

Wednesday night supper and the meetings. Everyone saw me there. I probably went home about nine thirty."

"Yes, Mr. White was killed after that hour."

Christine sucked in her breath with the realization they really did suspect her of murder. "I told you. I went home."

Detective Barton got up from the table and stood over the pastor. "Isn't your home right across the street from the church?"

Christine nodded.

"So you could easily return to the church after everyone was gone to murder Mr. White with no witnesses." Cole's eyes darkened. "Did you kill William White?"

Chapter Nine

Christine moved from desk to filing cabinet, gathering the files in preparation for the evening church administrative board meeting. Keeping busy helped take her mind off the interview at the police station that morning. Interview, they called it. It seemed more like an interrogation to her.

She dreaded the board meeting. It would be another discussion with members asking her questions about William and the investigation into his death. Rumors sprouted faster than the greening spring grass. The latest story making its way through the congregation was the local police staged the crime scene, so they could accuse someone of murder and be interviewed on the local and national news. It was true the story had been splashed across the country to satiate the never-ending enormous appetite to fill the hungry media's twenty-four hours a day, seven days a week news schedule.

Christine heard a knock on her closed office door. Unusual for it to be closed, but she had much to prepare for the meeting, including the denial that she had murdered William. Christine rolled her eyes. How could some of the congregants even think such a horrible story, let alone voice it and make up malicious rumors about her? Then she remembered her visit to the police station as a suspect, not as a pastor. That added fuel to the rumors for sure.

"Come in." She'd expected Ella to enter the office. Instead it was Dr. Harry Perkins, president of the board.

"Hi, Christine. I thought maybe we should get together for a minute before the meeting. We need to present a united front, don't you think?" The balding man stood in the open doorway watching her. He was dressed in a crisp plaid shirt and dark slacks. "I know it's been a tough week for you."

The pastor sat down heavily in her padded desk chair. "Well, I don't think it's been easy for anyone here. There's just too much focus on this death investigation. I think we should open up the meeting as usual with prayer and pray for William's family and for our church."

"Yes, I agree. We also need to pray for you and Dutch since the police are practically railroading you two into prison." The board president took the chair across the desk from Christine.

The investigation certainly was focusing on finding proof to incriminate Dutch and/or the pastor for William's murder. So far, not enough evidence had been processed to make a case against any one person.

Another knock at the door alerted them to the board secretary waiting outside.

"Come on in, Frank."

A lean man with snowy white hair entered

the room. The expensive dark suit and highly polished leather shoes distinguished Frank Parsons from many of the parishioners. The insurance salesman was always dressed impeccably from head to toe.

"Oh, I'm sorry to interrupt." Another knock at the door and another until all the officers of the board stood in Christine's office. Her heart swelled with this quiet assurance the board was affirming their belief in her innocence and showing their support by standing together, holding hands, and praying in the small office.

* * *

"Christine, Christine." Betty Jo Parsons scurried down the hall to join her after the meeting. "I know it's late, but may I talk to you privately for a minute?"

"Well, of course, Betty Jo. Come on in." She wondered why the chairman of the music committee needed to talk now. They'd hashed out plans to cover William's responsibilities at the admin board meeting earlier.

Betty Jo shut the office door behind her. "I didn't know who to tell. I have to tell somebody." The short, middle-aged woman weighed down by an enormous bosom looked intently into Christine's eyes.

"What is it, Betty Jo?" She came closer to the upset woman and placed her hand on her shoulder.

"I don't want to accuse anyone, or even

56

make a suggestion about someone…" The woman's gaze darted around the room, avoiding eye contact with Christine. "When I left the church the night of William's death, the Johnson's foster boy… I think his name is DeShawn? He went back into the church. I thought it was funny he was alone; his foster parents weren't around here. They'd probably walked home already. But why would DeShawn be here?"

Betty Jo fidgeted with the turquoise sweater draped across one arm. She finally fixed her gaze on her pastor and waited for an answer.

"Did you tell the police about this?"

"No, I didn't say anything because I didn't think it was important, but now with you and Dutch… Well, I don't want to get anyone in trouble." Her voice choked on the words. "I don't know what to do."

"Well you told me, and that's enough. I'm working with the police, and we'll let them handle it. Okay?" A look of relief flooded the worried woman's face. She slipped into her sweater and tried to button it across her ample bosom but gave up.

"Thank you, Pastor. You have a good night."

"You too. We'll soon put this behind us." Christine ushered her to the door. "God bless you, Betty Jo."

The pastor closed the door and turned to lean against it. She shook her head as the thought flashed across her mind. *Could Betty Jo be making something up to divert the police from her? But why would she want to kill William? Oh, Christine, get a grip. Don't be ridiculous.*

She closed her eyes and prayed. "God help us all."

* * *

"Good morning, Ella. Hello, Mason. How are you?" Whenever Christine saw Mason O'Leary, she couldn't help but think of an impish leprechaun with that sparkle of mischief in his eyes. Christine stepped into the church office with a smile on her face. She was determined the questioning at police headquarters yesterday was not going to ruin her day today.

"Well, you seem pretty cheery today. I have a few messages for you, but you just enjoy your coffee now." Ella picked up a tablet filled with notes.

"On a beautiful day like this, you have to be cheery. Say Ella, have I asked you if you want to take home a beautiful tiger cat to be your friend? Or maybe I should ask Mason?" She saw Mason's mouth turn up in a silly grin as he bobbed his shiny bald head up and down.

"Um, yes, about every morning for the past week, I'd say you mentioned it." Ella's eyes were full of mirth. The short cloud of white hair on her head complimented her round face, with features enhanced by perfectly applied make-up.

"And I'm assuming her answer is no for a cat. Correct, honey?" Mason interrupted, sneaking a look at his girlfriend, Ella.

Moving her hand to her forehead, she replied, "Yes, dear, you know me well enough to know the answer is no."

Christine watched as Ella and Mason exchanged loving glances, reminding her of goony-eyed teen-agers. Using his silver knobbed cane, the little man hobbled over to Ella and hugged her.

"Pastor, I wish you'd talk some sense into this woman's head. She will not set a wedding date. I'm ready to marry her tomorrow if she'd let me." Ella gently pushed Mason away from her. "Oh, Mason. Christine doesn't have time for this kind of stuff."

Christine shook her head. "No way I'm getting in the middle of this discussion." She watched the twinkle fade from his eyes.

"Here are your messages. Do you need anything else for the day?" Ella asked.

"Not that I can think of right now. Thanks." The pastor turned around to leave, then came back to Ella's desk. "What do you know about DeShawn, the Johnsons' foster boy?"

"Well, let's see. I think he's been with them for almost a year. His mom is in rehab, and the father isn't around here. His older brother is in jail. He's seen a lot for a teenage boy. Seems to be a nice kid. He's trying to fit in to the family."

"I think I'll go visit him after school this afternoon. Heading over to the nursing home this morning."

"Oh, yes, one of your messages is to call Lisa. She needs to re-schedule their pre-wedding counseling session. They can't make it at noon today."

"What? You mean I can eat lunch today? That's a change. Thanks, Ella. I'll see you later. Have a great day, Mason."

* * *

Christine couldn't make the decisions. The toppings for her sub sandwich all looked good. She knew it was the height of the rush hour, and people were waiting for her. Too many choices to enhance the turkey sandwich.

"Come on, Hobbs. Make up your mind. Mustard, mayo, pickles, white American cheese, lettuce, oil." Cole stood next to her, waiting for her to make her choices.

She glared at the pushy detective and then turned to the sandwich maker and said, "Yeah, all that plus tomato and onions."

"Good, finally. You can dress mine the same. No tomato and extra cheese."

Cole caught up with her at the drink station where she was debating about what pop to choose. "I imagine you're a diet cola drinker. May I pour?"

"Oh, thank you."

"Ah, you need some caffeine, eh, Preacher?" His eyes sparkled. She relaxed and returned his smile.

"I see you have your sandwich to go. Me, too. I'll meet you at the lakefront park for lunch at the picnic table under the big oak tree. Lots of shade and a beautiful view of the water."

"Oh, but I have…." She stopped to check her watch. No, she didn't have an appointment. She had the lunch hour free today. She had no excuse, and of course, a preacher couldn't tell a lie.

"Okay, I'll meet you there in a minute." What was she thinking? He's the man who was trying to send her to prison. Well, what could be wrong with having lunch with an attractive policeman? After all there was that saying. "Keep your friends close and your enemies closer."

* * *

The lake was just as beautiful and peaceful as Cole had described. The picnic table was available, and they both sat on one side facing the water. There was a vibrant feeling to the area. The lakeshore was recovering from the long, snowy winter of darkness and dormancy. It was a celebration of the returning warmth with green grass coloring the park area, birds chirping, tulips brightening the plantings, and green leaves popping from the branches. The bright blue sky and light breeze topped off the picture perfect weather.

The pair sat quietly for a while munching their sandwiches and sipping their drinks. She allowed the peace of the location to settle her.

"I'm sorry I had to be so tough on you in the interrogation room."

"Yeah, that was not a fun interview. You were all pretty rough on me, I'd say. I was getting a bit panicky, ready to call a lawyer."

"You don't know what tough is. That was a piece of cake compared to some interrogations of witnesses or suspects."

The wind whirled the napkins off the table. Both jumped to get them and bumped into each other. Electricity sizzled through her from his accidental touch.

"You probably can't tell me, but I'm still going to ask." She settled back on the bench of the picnic table. "Who do you think the murderer is?"

"Yeah, you're right. I can't tell you. Not cause I'm not supposed to. We just don't know. Everyone is still under suspicion. Even you, Preacher."

Christine's eyes widened in surprise. "I don't understand. Why would I be a suspect?"

"You were in the location and you have a motive. That leads us to you." Cole wiped his mouth with his napkin, then rolled up the waxed paper around his sandwich crumbs and napkin to make a tight ball. He aimed, tossed all of it toward the garbage can across the way, and made it. "Gotta go." He winked at her and stood up by the picnic table.

"Well, I was enjoying a pleasant lunch until now." Christine stared at the Detective. Handsome or not, she didn't like him accusing her of killing William.

She scooted out from the cramped picnic table and stood beside him.

He turned his palms upward and planted his feet in the green grass. "I have a job to do. I have to run down every possible lead."

Christine turned and stomped off to her car. The detective yelled toward her. "Hey, I didn't say you did it." But she wouldn't even turn back to look at him.

He stopped her as she opened the car door. "Christine, I have to check everything, so I can rule you out as the killer. Do you understand? It's my job."

She slid behind the wheel of her car, ignoring the cocky detective. Even slamming the car door shut to stop him from talking to her didn't relieve her frustration.

Out of the corner of her eye, Christine saw him shrug, then turn away to leave.

She sat quietly behind the steering wheel of her car with her eyes squeezed shut. *I don't know how, but I will find the killer. With God sustaining me, I'll prove Dutch and I are* not *guilty of murder.*

Chapter Ten

"The detective practically accused me of killing William, right there, right in the park." Sitting on the screened-in porch at the rear of the parsonage, Christine expected Lacey to be as angry as she was at such a ridiculous idea.

Instead, her friend held her slice of pizza midway from the greasy box to her mouth long enough to ask, "Hey, you didn't tell me you were at the park with Stephens this afternoon. How'd that happen?"

"What? You're more interested in why I was at the park instead of being accused of murdering William? Come on, Lacey." She planted her feet firmly on the cement floor and stopped the gentle rocking of the glider. "Don't you get it? I could be tossed in jail for something I didn't do."

"Don't be silly. You're innocent. You know it, and so does everyone else." Lacey popped the last morsel of pepperoni in her mouth. "Anyway, tell me how you met Cole Stephens at the park." Her friend licked the pizza grease from her fingers and then grabbed the thin paper napkin to complete the grease removal from her lips.

"Excuse me, Lacey. Some people in this town are spreading rumors that I killed William.

I wouldn't be surprised if it weren't some of my own parishioners involved in spreading them. There were several folks who weren't too happy to have a young woman for their pastor."

"You don't think they'd spread malicious lies to get you out of here, do you?"

"I hope not." Christine sat back on the glider and sipped her light beer. She was too upset to eat the pizza Lacey had brought over.

"I guess we could always do our own investigation, eh?" She threw it out there to get a reaction from her friend.

"Sure, Sherlock." Lacey laughed. "We could go to William's house to see if someone left a note telling us who killed him."

Christine sat bolt upright. "You're right! We could run out there and investigate."

"I'm sure the police have already done that. There's nothing left to check out." Lacey piled the paper napkins next to the half empty pizza box on the patio table.

They sat in silence for a few minutes allowing the peaceful twilight to restore tranquility. Christine couldn't let go of the idea of checking out William's home. After all, William had shown her where the key was if she needed to get into his house in case of an emergency. *I think trying to find William's killer could qualify as an emergency.*

Christine moved to the patio table. "We've got to go to William's house and look for clues to his killer."

"We can't even get into his house."

"Oh yes, we can. I know where he hides his house key. Come on, let's go." Christine swooped up the pizza box and bottles.

"Hey, what about the pizza?"

"I'll store it in my refrigerator for a midnight snack. Let's go now." Christine was fired up to prove her innocence. Sitting back and waiting to find out who murdered William was no longer an option. She needed to take action toward solving this mystery, so she and her congregation could deal with it and move forward.

* * *

Christine and Lacey pulled into the gravel driveway of the small, neat house William rented and parked her car in the back. Groves of mature oak trees graced the front and back yards of the spacious property, shielding the amateur investigators from being noticed by travelers on the road. The landscaping around the house was a work of art, lovingly designed, planted, and nurtured by William.

It was a clear, starry night with a full moon that helped to light the yard. The spring air had turned cold, but Christine was warm with the anticipation of finding something in the house that would prove she was not a murderer and also clear Dutch from any possible murder charges.

"The police probably padlocked the doors and have cameras watching the house," Lacey whined.

The two women crouched as they snuck up to the back porch of the house. Christine flashed her light on the door. No padlock in sight.

"Hmmph," she said. "No padlock, so I'm sure there are no cameras here." She turned and winked at Lacey. "I just hope William hasn't moved his keys."

She stepped into the landscaped area surrounding the small pool and fountain. Christine picked up a large paver from those covering the edge of the pool liner and flashed her light over the ground. "Uh-oh, it isn't here. Let me try another one." She lifted three more pavers until she pulled up a small coffee can buried in the dirt. Returning the pavers to their proper position, she brought the container back to Lacey who waited on the sidewalk.

She handed her flashlight to Lacey and pulled the lid away from the container. "Light up the inside of this can. I don't know what may be inside."

The light revealed no dirt, bugs, worms, or varmints, so Christine put her hand in to pull out the set of keys.

"Here's our ticket into the house." She looked through the collection of keys on the key ring and then plugged one into the lock on the door. Trying not to breathe too deeply of the stench emanating from the trash bags on the screened-in porch, she tested another key until it turned, making a loud click. The women slipped quietly into the kitchen.

"Chris." She felt Lacey's hand on her shoulder. "I just want to make sure you realize we are breaking and entering. We could go to jail for this."

"Well, this is no time to debate if this is breaking and entering or not. We're here. Trust me." Christine winked.

She scanned the spotlessly cleaned room. It was never that clean when she had visited his home. His sister must have already been here or hired a crew to go through the house. "Come on. I'll take the bedrooms and bathroom. You search the rest of the house."

"What am I looking for?" Lacey held her hands out to her sides, then shrugged.

"Look for notes, books, journals, appointments and anything that might be out of character for William. I don't know for sure, Lacey. I'm new at this investigation thingy, too."

"Um, okay. Let's stay together. It's creepy sneaking around in someone's home in the dark. Okay?" Lacey put her arm around Christine's shoulders.

"Okay, we're in this together." Christine moved toward the living room and began the search.

The women spent over an hour looking through closets, shelves, and drawers. They peeked under the couch cushions and under the beds. After checking out every nook and cranny of the small house, Christine finally sat down on the couch.

"It looks like William's sister was very efficient in cleaning out the house," said Lacey, "and erasing any evidence William ever lived here."

"There's only one more thing we haven't checked, Lacey."

Their eyes locked, and they both said, "The trash."

"Oh, no way." Lacey wrinkled up her nose. "I'm not digging through that stinky garbage on the porch."

"Aw, come on. You know you'll love it." Grinning big, Christine jumped up from the couch and grabbed Lacey's hand. Tugging her toward the back porch, Christine said, "I owe you big for this."

"Oh, yes, you do, and I expect to collect big, too."

The very ripe bags of trash stood on the back porch waiting for pick up. The amateur sleuths dragged them into the kitchen and sorted through them. Discovering the usual kitchen waste in one, lots of yogurt containers, whole wheat bread wrapper, vegetable peelings, rotting apple cores, and the remnants of cereal and cracker boxes, they plowed through the second black bag.

It contained articles from William's bathroom and office, soap box, toilet paper roll, deodorant, music catalogs, notes and figures scribbled on a music company order form, a blank order form with Joanie's name circled on it, receipts, and a collection of ball point pens and pencils in various degrees of sharpness. Pushing everything back into the bags, they hauled them back to the porch.

"We're missing something. What is it?" She moved to the living room. Lacey joined her in the middle of the room.

Headlight beams flashed through the front window of the house. They dove behind the couch. Christine couldn't breathe. Lacey trembled beside her. The gravel crunched on the driveway as the vehicle backed out and headed down the road in the opposite direction. Crouching behind the couch, the would-be investigators waited for someone to walk in and discover them.

"Do you think they dropped someone off here?" Lacey whispered.

"I think if they were coming in, we would've heard the car door slam by now."

Holding her breath, she heard nothing but silence. No one coming in.

"We might as well lock up the house and get out of here. We may be pushing our luck," Christine bravely peeked over the back of the couch toward the front window, then stood up, a bit shaken.

"Wait a minute. We never checked inside the refrigerator. You know people always hide stuff in the freezer. At least that's the way it is in the movies." Lacey headed to the small kitchen shining her flashlight to find the way. Chris rolled her eyes then followed anyway.

Lacey opened the freezer compartment with

a flourish. "Aha." She shined her light inside the empty freezer.

"What did you find?" Christine crowded into her at the refrigerator door.

"Nothing." Lacey turned and grinned. "I guess that only happens in the movies, eh?" She closed the freezer door. If anyone would have told me we would be out here trying to prove you innocent of a murder, breaking and entering into William's house, or that you had lunch with Cole Stephens at the park, I would've told 'em they were crazy."

She had to agree with Lacey. "Yeah, you're right. It's all crazy. However, the really unbelievable part was I met Cole at the park." Laughing, Christine pushed Lacey toward the door. The search at William's house was a bust. Or was it? She felt like they'd missed something. What was it?

She hoped Cole would never find out about this desperate act. Lacey wouldn't tell anyone. Besides, Christine didn't want to see that detective again. Or did she?

Chapter Eleven

Wednesday night was Christine's favorite night of the week. She could mingle with her congregation at the supper held in the basement of the church. It was an evening of good food, Bible studies, choir practices, and fellowship as a community of believers.

"How's choir practice going, Betty Jo?"

The woman's weak smile told Christine the story. "We can't seem to get our hearts into it. Little things remind us of William all the time. Sorrow has overcome our spirit."

"Would it help if I joined you before your practice tonight? Maybe a little pep talk and clearing the air?" She wanted to help this group of dedicated people cope with the loss.

"Oh, yes, please join us." Betty Jo smiled.

"All right, I'll see you in a few minutes." Christine continued to walk around the tables where the parishioners were eating the meal the men's group had prepared for this evening. She caught pieces of conversation as she moved around the room.

"Well, yes, I heard William was into gambling and owed a bundle to the mafia," said one diner.

"Poor Dutch. He must've snapped."

"You know, even the pastor is under investigation," stated a woman who stabbed the air with her fork with each word spoken.

Christine made no acknowledgement of the conversations she overheard. Instead she portrayed a positive, upbeat attitude by mingling with her parishioners. She entered the choir room which was, as usual, a bit chaotic with members greeting each other, passing out sheet music, and a group pecking out an exceptionally difficult passage on the piano.

"Hello, everyone." She hoped her voice carried over all the cacophony of sounds and voices. They stopped to listen, and eventually she had the attention of each person.

"I understand William's passing has been difficult for all of us. I know losing him has hit you folks very hard. You've spent a lot of hours together with William, practicing the music you all love."

She stopped to look at the diversity of the group. Teen-agers to senior citizens, lawyers, real estate sales people, factory workers, teachers, waitresses, and more. Some were new members, and others had been contributing to the choir for forty years. No matter their ages, work backgrounds, ethnic group, or even their expertise in music, they met every week to practice singing for God and to bring God's spirit into church every Sunday. That was a commitment each had made and being here this evening only showed their determination to keep it.

"Can you feel the presence of William here with us? He's still directing us to do the best we can to share God's love through the joy of music with our congregation, to allow God's spirit to shine through us when singing in the worship service and in our everyday lives. We'll never forget William and what he has brought to us and to our music. Let's keep his memory alive in our hearts and in our music."

A clear soprano voice began singing one of William's favorite hymns, "Be Still My Soul." Spontaneously the choir members joined the one voice until the rich, beautiful sounds soared through the choir room. They clasped their hands together and formed a circle as they sang the song of prayer and faith.

"Amen. Amen," whispered Pastor Christine as the last notes of the song faded.

* * *

Nothing was going well for Christine on Thursday afternoon. Slumping in her office chair, she felt exhausted.

She tried answering e-mails, but her mind felt thick. The day was barely half over, and she was too tired to even put three words together to make a sentence. She hadn't slept well since learning of William's murder and was sick of the unrelenting media sensationalizing the story every night on the news.

A knock at her door interrupted her moment of rest. "Come on in."

"I hated to bother you again. You look exhausted, Pastor." Ella popped in the room dressed in her stylish suit of spring green. Eyeglasses dangling from a beaded necklace bobbed against her bosom.

"I'm dragging today." She couldn't tell Ella about snooping around at William's house late at night, or that last night's activities at the church and the stress of being accused of murder were piling up on her.

"I was checking in to see if you had the scripture reading figured out for Sunday. I'll be working on the bulletin this afternoon."

"Oh, yes, here it is, Ella. I'm sorry I didn't get it to you sooner. The days are flying by."

"Thank you. Have you talked with Detective Stephens lately?" Concern filled Ella's face.

"Not really. I think he's pretty busy. It sounds like he's interviewed practically the whole church by now. I've talked with quite a few folks who are upset the police are questioning everyone."

"I agree. It was no fun re-living that day when I was interviewed." Ella sighed. "I wonder if they have gleaned any information about the killer from all the interviews. I'm just asking because I know this is taking a toll on you. I just want it to be cleared up."

"Oh, me, too. I wish I knew more about William. What went wrong in his life? So wrong that it killed him?" Christine thought about William's situation. "Can you think of anything we've missed? I know this sounds crazy." Christine leaned in to the desk and quietly asked. "Could his sister be a part of his mysterious death?"

Ella's eyes grew wide. "Oh, Pastor. I have no idea. I only met her a few times. He didn't talk much about his family."

"Oh, please, forgive me for suggesting such an idea. I guess I'm grasping at straws for an explanation." She picked up the paper with the scripture reading and title of the sermon and handed it to the secretary.

"Thank you." Ella turned the paper in her hand and put on her glasses to read it. Then she quietly asked, "Did you want to put that notice in the bulletin about finding a new home for your cat?"

"Oh come on now, when you say she's my cat, are you trying to dissuade me from giving her away? I just don't feel I give her enough time. I'm never home lately."

"Umm…okay. Is that a yes for the notice then?" Ella's grin reminded Christine of the Cheshire cat in *Alice's Adventures in Wonderland*.

"I guess. Well, let me think about it another week. I really don't have time to take care of a cat. Yeah, give me another week. Thanks, Ella."

Christine dug through her bag to find a piece of gum. She pushed her wallet to the side and pulled out William's keys. It dawned on her that in their haste to leave, she'd forgotten to bury the keys back in the coffee can. Now what should she do with them?

She looked through the assortment of keys

on the ring and recognized keys to the church, probably to the church office, William's office, filing cabinet, his car. Christine looked again. She held the keys to William's office and files.

No, I shouldn't. Um, no I can't.

She sent a text to Lacey. *Meet me at my house tonight at ten o'clock.*

Chapter Twelve

Under a star-filled sky, Lacey and Christine silently proceeded across the blacktop parking lot to enter the church. "I don't get it. What do you need me for?"

"I need you to help me with the search." She unlocked the back door, and the two amateur sleuths slipped inside. They jumped when they heard the familiar clank as the door closed and locked behind them. In the quiet darkness, the sound reverberated throughout the hallway.

Lacey cringed. "Shhhh." She turned on her flashlight. "No noise, no lights...otherwise it's like lighting up a neon sign announcing, 'Your Pastor is Now In. Come and See Her.'" Lacey's fingers made a frame in the air.

"Agreed." Christine nodded. She switched on her flashlight to illuminate the dark hallway.

"Okay, Sherlock. What are we searching for? What's your plan?" Lacey asked in a hushed voice.

"First we're going to check out the basement where they found William's body." Christine took a deep breath. "Then we're going into William's office and look into his files and go through the choir room shelves and files. Now do you see why I need you to help me?"

Lacey stopped in the middle of the hall. "Okay. Can you clue me in to what we're looking for?"

"Well, I'm not sure yet. We'll know it when we see it," Christine replied.

Lacey rolled her eyes. "Oh my gosh, we're searching for something, and we have no idea what we're looking for?" Lacey slapped her hand on her forehead. "This reminds me too much of the search at William's house where we ended up with zilch information. We're going to spend hours searching, and we don't even know what we are looking for…again." Lacey stood firm with hands on her hips.

"Lacey, please. I have to do something to prove, if not my own innocence, but for Dutch and his family. There has to be something to help us and the police find the killer."

"I guess when you explain it that way." Lacey motioned with her flashlight. "Okay. I'm ready."

She opened the door to the stairs leading to the basement furnace room. The beam from her flashlight lit the stairwell. A lump forged in her throat knowing William had plunged to his death here.

Lacey followed her down the narrow wooden stairs. "These don't seem slippery or broken."

Christine stopped on the steps and turned. "You have to remember. William did not fall down these stairs. It wasn't an accident. He was murdered and either thrown down after he was killed or died on impact at the bottom." The two continued down the steep stairway, stepped on the landing, turned, and finished their descent in silence.

At the bottom of the steps, the pastor took a deep breath and closed her eyes breathing a silent prayer for courage and strength. The room brought back the memory of seeing William's body sprawled out on the tiled floor and his head in a pool of blood. She would never be able to erase that grisly image from her mind.

The lock to the choir room door clicked when Christine turned the key. Taking a deep breath, she pushed open the wooden door. Lacey followed her. The lights from the women's flashlights illuminated the room set up with rows of chairs for the choir members placed in a semi-circle. The Spinet piano graced the front of the room, and William's music stand remained in its position in front of the choir's seats. This time, his baton was not lying across the bottom of it waiting for him to lift it and lead the choir. The choir director would never return to use the baton again.

As she gazed around the space, she noticed closet doors open revealing nothing stored in them. The shelves and cabinets were empty of the usual clutter, music, and William's fun figures of musical instruments. The music director's computer was missing from his large wooden desk as well as his basket files. The desk and filing cabinet drawers gaped open on their tracks.

Lacey stopped behind Christine. "Who in the world cleaned all the stuff out of here? Surely William's sister couldn't have done this, too?"

"The police. The police were down here looking for evidence. I knew they carried out some of the things. I had no idea they took everything."

Christine pushed a sliding closet door back on its track to look more closely. "The cases of hand bells and chimes are gone. They even took the box of the kids' old rhythm band instruments." Her eyes misted over when she recalled how excited he had been about ordering new ones to replace the well-used and broken ones for his kids' choir. They had discussed the expense and how to pay for it. Her eyes misted over at the memory. They never did meet with Joanie to discuss paying for the expenditure by using some monies from the music department and from the Christian education funds.

She stood up and turned to Lacey. "I'm sorry to drag you out tonight on this wild goose chase. It's disheartening. I was so sure there would be something here."

"Hey, you didn't know they'd clean the place out. I mean it's kinda good in a way. At least the police are looking for evidence to find the killer. They're doing something." Lacey put her hand on Christine's shoulder. "After all, you aren't a detective. You don't know police procedure. Chalk it up to a learning experience."

"Yeah, well, I hope it's not a lesson I'll

ever have to use again."

The two women walked toward the door to leave.

"I still can't believe William's gone." Lacey turned around to look at the empty room before she walked into the hall. "I hope they catch whoever murdered him…and soon."

Christine pulled the door shut and checked to make sure the choir room door locked.

"I'm sure he was never married. His sister was his only family."

"He always ordered flowers for Christmas and her birthday. He loved flowers." Lacey's voice broke.

Christine placed her arm around Lacey's shoulders. "We have to do everything we can to find out who killed William to clear Dutch. Besides, the murderer could be hunting someone else. We've got to find him before he kills again."

Not wishing to use the stairwell again where William had fallen, they made their way down the dark hallway leading to the elevator to take them to the main floor.

Christine stopped and listened. "Don't move. Someone's using the elevator."

Chapter Thirteen

The gentle whirring motor signaled the descent of the elevator. Christine and Lacey froze. *Who would be in the church basement at this time of night? Maybe it was the killer coming back for something.*

Lacey pulled her to the bathroom door across from the elevator, and they squeezed through the doorway allowing it to close softly behind them. Neither of them breathed.

Footsteps signaled someone's exit from the elevator. No hallway light shone through the crack under the door. Quick steps scurried off down the hall.

"What do we do now?" Christine heard Lacey's hushed whisper but couldn't see her in the dark bathroom.

"I guess we either wait till whoever it is gets back on the elevator, or turn on the hallway light and see who's here."

"Well, I vote for getting out of this bathroom and finding out what's going on," Lacey said.

"Okay, let's go."

The two women opened the door and slipped out. Heart thudding in her chest, Christine found the light switch in the hallway and flipped it on. The fluorescent lights practically blinded them after the pitch blackness in the bathroom.

Lacey held her flashlight like a baseball bat, ready to clobber anyone who might show up. "Whoever got out of the elevator should know we're here now."

"Evidently our visitor doesn't want to be seen," Christine said. "Come on. He can't be too far away from us."

"That's what I'm afraid of." Lacey followed behind her.

Using the lights from the hall and their flashlights, it was easy to see no one was in the fellowship room or adjacent kitchen.

The choir room door was still locked when Lacey tried the doorknob, so all that was left to check was the classroom and furnace room. When Christine threw open the door of the classroom, someone with the force of a freight train barreled through the doorway, knocking them down on the hard tiled floor.

Lacey moaned behind her. Christine switched on the light and found her lying flat on the floor holding her head. No one else was in sight.

She squatted down beside her dazed friend. "Are you okay?" She tried to look at Lacey's head, except her injured ally swatted her hands away.

"I'm fine. My head bounced off the floor when I fell." She touched the side of her head. No blood. "Ouch. I think I'm going to have a big lump and a headache though."

"Shall I call 9-1-1? I'm concerned you might have a concussion."

"No, no, I told you I'm fine," Lacey said.

Christine helped her to her feet. "Well, we sure showed him, didn't we? I think he was more afraid of us the way he took off."

"Do you think he's gone?"

"Yes, I heard him pounding up the steps and the door open and slam shut. He's gone all right." Christine, with hands on hips, said, "Huh...afraid of two women."

Lacey didn't even smile at the feeble joke. She felt her head again. "Come on, let's call it a night. Do you want me to stay at your place tonight, or do you want to come on home with me?"

"Oh, I'm fine. I don't need anyone to stay with me." Christine pulled the classroom door shut. *But maybe I should be with you to make sure you don't have a concussion.*

"You're not worried that whoever is here in the church will come to the parsonage?"

"Well, I wasn't until you just said that! You're welcome to stay tonight. I'll get some ice for your head, and then I can put a frozen pizza in the oven." Christine grinned. "This detective work makes me hungry."

"I'll come," Lacey gently rubbed the forming knot on her head, "not because of the frozen pizza offer. Even the idea of it offends my gourmet pizza sensibilities."

Chapter Fourteen

Christine covered her mouth with her hand to stifle a yawn and vowed the late nights had to stop. She sat in her desk chair pouring over pages in her commentary. She had to get the sermon written. The *Bible* scripture she'd chosen demanded more study to answer all the questions it provoked.

The notes she had jotted on the points in the sermon weren't flowing smoothly into a meaningful lesson. She'd put off finalizing the message till the last minute, and now nothing seemed to work. Too many interruptions, too many stressed out people, too many questions, and too many thoughts of Cole Stephens.

Why am I thinking of the detective? The thought of him gave her goose bumps as she remembered the sizzle she felt when they touched accidentally at the picnic table in the park. She recalled how his dark lashes framed his warm, brown eyes. She rubbed her eyes to erase the attractive picture of him in her mind. Then again, wasn't he trying to prove she murdered William?

She welcomed the knock on her office door to get her mind off of Cole. "Come in."

The door opened only halfway revealing a stocky man dressed in jeans and red plaid flannel shirt. He peeked around the edge of the door. "Hi,

Pastor. I hate to interrupt you. Do you have a minute?"

"Oh, come on in, Jackson." He ambled into the office. She stood up and offered her hand to greet him. After a firm handshake, he remained in front of the desk and nervously twirled his baseball cap in his fingers. Christine tried to recall how she met Jackson. Oh yes, he was the kind man who helped her unload donations to the community yard sale last spring.

"Thank you for letting me stop in. I have some folks I'd like you to meet. They're having some hard times. Can you talk to them? They're out in my van waiting."

"What kind of problems?" She tried to move the conversation along, so she could return to finish writing her sermon. Time was flying by.

"Well, I really wish you could come and talk to them about their situation. I really want to help them out, but I don't know how to do it."

"Oh, sure. Please have them come in." Christine smiled.

"Well, it might be a little easier for you to come on out to the parking lot, ma'am." He bobbed his head apologetically.

Christine glanced out her window at Jackson's dusty navy blue van. Rust spidered its way around the bottom of the vehicle and outlined the doors. She imagined the van had seen a lot of miles and a lot of hunting trips.

"Well, what's happened to these folks that you need to help them out?" She motioned to him to take a seat as she returned to her chair.

Jackson eased his round body into the chair across from her desk. "Well, ya' see, I met these folks in the campground out there on White Lake, a few miles west of here. There's a great fishin' hole and this and that. Anyways, we were camped there, never knew them from Adam till we met a week ago. He's a fisherman, too."

She nodded, listening intently, wishing he'd get to the point of the story.

"Well, this mornin', ya'see, something popped in their motor home, and before we knew it, their motor home went up in flames. It couldn't have took more than a minute, and now it's a burned out wreck."

"Oh, no. Did anyone get hurt?" Christine leaned forward in her chair.

"No, thank the good Lord, we was all outside at my place havin' coffee. The problem is they lost everything. Their wallets, credit cards, clothes....you name it. All gone. They couldn't save nothin'. They only have the clothes on their backs. I told 'em we'd come and see you 'cause you'd know how to help them get back home to Tennessee."

"Oh yes, there are agencies to help them right here in the county. Just a minute." She dug through her desk for a business card from the social worker at the human services agency. "You know where this agency is located, don't you, Jackson?"

"Sure, I do. Will you come out and meet these folks? They're pretty upset."

Resigned that Jackson would not leave unless

she agreed to meet with the distressed couple, Christine stood up from her desk and smiled. "I'd be happy to meet them."

When the pastor and Jackson emerged from the church, an older man, short and paunchy, slowly climbed out from the passenger side of the van. He limped to the sliding door and opened it up. He helped a woman who looked as squishy as a marshmallow, soft and round, clamber out of the van. The bulky woman wore a brightly colored print shirt, neon green cardigan sweater, and pink polyester slacks with matching pink clogs.

She turned and reached inside the van. Christine blinked to make sure she was clearly seeing the lady gently lift what looked like a pig on a leash onto the asphalt parking lot. The man went around to the back of the van, opened the door, and a small kangaroo on a harness hopped out of the vehicle.

Christine stopped in her tracks. "Am I seeing what I think I'm seeing?" She looked at Jackson, then back to the van. She closed her eyes and then re-opened them, trying to convince her brain the scene was real.

"Pastor, this here is Harley and his friend, Iola." Christine shook their hands, getting a whiff of stale cigar smoke mixed with bacon grease.

"And who are these delightful creatures?" She wanted to pinch herself to be sure this wasn't a dream. What an odd assortment of pets. All in a camper?

"Oh, this here is Katy, our kangaroo, well, I guess she's really what ya' call a wallaby, and

Abraham, our pot-bellied pig."

Christine stooped to pat the pig's head and then scratched around his ears. The gentle swine, big as a medium sized dog, grunted with pleasure. Assured by the sounds and smell of the pig this was not a dream, she couldn't help but smile at the outrageous family.

"I'm sorry you're having such a tough time. I hated to hear about your RV fire. I told Jackson about an agency that can help you."

"Thank you, thank you so much, Pastor." When Christine stood up, Harley pumped her hand again. "Iola is so upset. She's practically hysterical. She's so worried about how we're gonna get back home. We can't even rent a car without a proper driver's license. Everything burned up in the fire." Tears puddled in his gray eyes.

Suddenly the pig began grunting and straining at the leash, dancing around as if on a bed of hot coals.

"Oooooh, Harley, my nitro." Iola clutched her chest and then fell to the ground like a limp rag doll.

"Darlin', darlin'!" Harley moved as quickly as a teen-ager to cradle his unconscious girlfriend in his arms. He dug in his shirt pocket to find the medicine. "Iola, honey!" The pig moved into the scene, grunting and prodding the supine woman.

Christine ran to the church door and yelled at Ella, "Ella, Ella, call 9-1-1. A woman collapsed in the parking lot." She raced back to the scene where Jackson had already started CPR on the lifeless woman. Christine pulled off her suit coat and placed it under Iola's head, then shot a quick prayer to heaven.

Ella rushed out of the office with the handheld phone to her ear. She pulled up short when she saw the scene before her, then rushed toward the group and yelled. "They're on the way now!"

Taking a few steps toward Christine, she asked, "Is there something else I can do?" Her eyebrows raised high up to her forehead as she surveyed the animals and the woman on the pavement held gently by the man.

"Oh thanks, Ella. Just watch for the ambulance."

"Um, okay. I never was much help with animals." She backed away from the scene with her eyes on Abraham and Katy."

Harley returned the vial of nitro glycerin tablets, always kept close to his heart, to his shirt pocket. Unbelievably, the kangaroo stood next to his owner and didn't try to escape.

* * *

Christine watched the EMTs load Iola into the ambulance and secure the cot inside. Harley boosted up the pig, shoved him into the back of the ambulance, and started to grab the kangaroo.

The EMT stuck his head out the back door. "Hold on there. Wait a minute. Sir, we can't be taking a pig to the hospital and for sure, not that kangaroo either. You've gotta leave them here."

Flashing a glance at Christine, the EMT rolled his eyes and shook his head. "Hurry up, sir. We've got to get this patient to the hospital."

Harley pulled Abraham out of the ambulance. Grabbing the pig and the kangaroo's leashes, he quickly handed them off to Christine, then hoisted himself into the back of the ambulance with help from the EMT. The siren started wailing as the lime green ambulance lumbered its way out of the parking lot onto the road and toward the intersection.

Christine stood in the parking lot hanging onto the leash of the agitated pig in one hand and the docile kangaroo in the other. Taking her eyes from the ambulance careening out of the parking lot, she turned her attention to the animals and wondered what just happened here.

Her heart caught in her throat when she spotted Cole Stephens speed into the parking lot, barely missing the departing ambulance. *What was he doing here?*

He pulled up near her and jumped from the car. "I heard the call come through. I was afraid of what I'd discover at this church."

His serious expression broke out into a huge smile. "You never know what situation a 9-1-1 call will lead to. This… this is a first for me." His hearty laughter echoed off the brick walls of the building. "He wiped tears of laughter from his eyes with the back of his hand.

Cole's appearance seemed to shake up the animals. Christine struggled to hang on to them, so the detective grabbed the kangaroo's harness and tried to calm the frightened animal.

"What are you doing with the Noah's ark critters?" She saw the twinkle in his eyes. Her face cracked into a smile. She had to admit it was an odd situation. She must look like an idiot standing out in the lot hanging onto these two adorable creatures.

"Well, in a nutshell. A woman had a cardiac arrest here in the parking lot. As you saw, she's on her way to the hospital, and well, these are her pets." Christine swept her free hand toward the animals just catching a glimpse of Jackson's old van making a beeline for the parking lot exit.

"Isn't that right, Ella?"

"Yes, her pets." Ella nodded and pointed to Katy and Abraham.

"Um, I guess I'm keeping them till, well, until... Let's just say we didn't really have time to discuss it. I'm sure you probably have a place to put them, don't you?"

"Huh-uh, lady. I'm not taking in any animals." He backed away as if they were wild animals ready to attack. "Anyway, my retriever would probably eat them." His wink was disarming.

Christine turned to Ella standing nearby. "Ella, would you?"

"No way, Pastor. You're on your own with those animals. Remember? I'm the one who didn't even want the cat." Ella made a quick exit for the safety of the church office.

Christine turned to the detective. "Now what am I going to do?" She pushed her bangs off her forehead.

"I can call the animal shelter. They'll probably take them. Meanwhile, shall we take them over to the parsonage lawn instead of standing here?" He tugged a bit on the kangaroo's leash.

Katy didn't exactly hop right. She had a hitch in her hop gait. What a sight as the little band hopped, tugged, pulled their way across the street and into the back yard.

"Do you think this animal is housebroken?" Cole asked.

Christine sliced her gaze at Cole ready to dress him down while she was in the middle of this predicament until she spotted those sparkling eyes full of mischief. A grin spread across her face. "Well I don't think the congregation would appreciate a kangaroo in the parsonage, nor a pig. Would you call the shelter for me now, please?"

"Sure." He slipped his phone off his belt.

Thank goodness Katy and Abraham needed her attention. Otherwise she would've cupped his face in her hands and given him a healthy kiss for being here with her.

For the first time, she had a chance to pet and soothe the homeless animals. *Why would anyone want to go camping with a pig and a kangaroo?* When she looked at Abraham, she noticed his eyes were milky. She waved her hand on one side of his head and then the other. He didn't flinch. Abraham was blind.

"Bad news, Pastor. The shelter won't take them. They're not equipped for these animals, and there's some kind of health department licenses that would be in jeopardy. Looks like you're in charge, Ms. Noah." He grinned.

"Well, this is just great. Just wonderful. I'm going to make some calls. Surely there are some farmers who could take them."

"Hold on. Don't you think you can just wait awhile? Maybe the owner will be back tonight and take them home."

"Yes, if he had a home to take them back to." Christine relayed the whole story to Cole as they constructed a makeshift fence for the pig and tethered the kangaroo in the back yard.

"I don't even know what to feed a kangaroo." Christine's eyes widened at the realization.

"Well, we can talk to the owner and then go shopping for pig and kangaroo food." After he said it, they both laughed at the ridiculous situation. "First, we go for a burger," he suggested.

"All right. It's a deal." She felt her face light up when she gazed at Cole. The knit shirt hugged his muscular chest. She wanted to run her fingers across his five o'clock shadow. Maybe she had misjudged him after all.

Chapter Fifteen

"I'm glad you're feeling better, Iola." Christine stood by the bedside of the pale woman.

"It's my old ticker, Pastor. It gets weaker and weaker. Thank goodness for Abraham. He's my service pig. He alerts us before I know I'm having an attack. I don't understand how he knows, but he does."

"Yes, Abraham certainly did his job. Now why do you have Katy? Is she trained to alert you, too, or is she just an exotic pet?" Christine's eyes sparkled in anticipation of the answer to this question. At dinner she and Cole had tossed around reasons why anyone would want a kangaroo.

"Oh, my dear, dear Katy. Such a loving animal. She's trained to signal Harley when he's going to have a seizure. It gives him time to sit or lie down before he seizes. He's had quite a few injuries from falls. Thank goodness the animals always have their radar working." Iola's big smile revealed her gums, no teeth.

"Well, I've heard of service dogs, never pigs and kangaroos."

"You know they really are our pets now, too." Iola stopped to catch her breath. She grabbed the oxygen mask from the bed rail and put it back over her nose and mouth. "I hate this thing, but it does help. Sorry, Pastor."

"Oh, that's all right. Don't be too anxious to get rid of it if you need it to breathe." She reached to help her but Iola was already adjusting it on her face.

"Katy and Abraham have been our family for many years. Harley's boys are scattered around the country, and my daughter, well, me and her don't get along too good. So it's just Harley and me, Abraham and Katy." Iola's hands lay limply at her side, one arm pierced with the IV tube. Other cables connected her to the machine that registered her blood pressure readings. Her middle finger sported a high tech clothespin-looking clip to read her oxygen levels.

"I'm not worried about the animals. I know you'll take real good care of them till I'm outta here." Iola flashed her toothless smile again.

"I'll be glad to keep them tonight for you. Tomorrow, I'll make arrangements with one of the farmers in the congregation to take care of them till you can go home." She patted Iola's shoulder gently.

"Oh, Pastor Christine, you can't send them out to a farm, leaving them in a barn with other animals. They could get sick, or bitten, or who knows what dangers there are. Promise me you won't do that, please." Christine saw the blood pressure reading increase on the machine.

"Don't worry. I'll take good care of them." The pastor bit her lip. *Now why did I say that?*

"Harley told me what those guys eat. I'm leaving here to go food shopping for them. I'd better get going, so you can rest up for those tests tomorrow."

"Thank you, Pastor. Thank you so much. Before you go, can you say a prayer for me and Harley, and be sure to include Abraham and Katy?" Iola blinked away the tears.

Christine took Iola's hand and squeezed it. "Let's pray."

* * *

Christine unloaded the plastic bags full of supplies for her overnight guests out of the trunk of her car. The bags were packed with water bowls and food bowls that wouldn't get dumped over, or so the clerk at the pet store told her. Another bag was stuffed with fresh fruit and raw vegetables. Cole hoisted a fifty-pound bag of feed over his shoulder, carrying it like it was no heavier than a feather.

After getting the items all dished up for the animals, she and Cole stepped out of the way. Katy scarfed down the fresh veggies. Abraham only sniffed at the food from the feed store.

"It's okay, Abraham." Christine squatted down and petted the pig. "Iola is going to be just fine. You'll be with her real soon...I hope." She looked at Cole and rolled her eyes.

"Hey, big guy, eat up. We didn't run our asses off around town just so you could turn up your nose at it." Cole bent over and scratched the pig between his ears. He dropped a red apple into the bowl. After a few grunts, Abraham chomped it down.

"Say, I think you have a way with pigs." She giggled and stood up. She and Cole were about the same height with Cole edging her out by a smidgen.

"Yeah, I'm a winner with a pig but not the preacher lady, I guess." His funny smile made her feel a bit dizzy.

"Oh, please. I'm sure you have a harem of women after you."

Cole shrugged off her comment on their way back to his car in the parsonage driveway.

"Thank you so much for helping me with the animals." She put her hand out for a shake. Cole held her hand much longer than necessary for a handshake.

Electricity surged through her body as he pulled her closer. She was drawn into his seductive eyes. The fragrance of his cologne added even more spice to the moment. Although she yearned to be in his arms, she stepped back from him, afraid of her feelings.

"I'll call you." His husky voice was quiet in the fading evening light.

"Okay. I look forward to that. Thanks again."

He backed his black Dodge Ram pickup out of the driveway. Christine watched him drive away, wishing she could call him back. She remained standing in the darkness still staring at the empty road. *What is it about that man?* One minute he was practically accusing her of murder, and the next, he was so sweet and caring. She chuckled out loud when she recalled him chasing the gimpy kangaroo for her. Yes, he was an enigma she wanted to investigate.

Chapter Sixteen

In her driveway on Saturday morning, Christine sprayed down her car with the hose as she hummed her favorite hymn since childhood, "This Is My Father's World." The big bucket of warm, soapy water sat near the passenger side front tire next to a bag of rags. A warm breeze, a little shade from the tall oak near the driveway, and time to make her beloved SUV shine added to her good mood. She slopped the soapy water on the hood of the vehicle and hummed as she scrubbed.

"Hi, Pastor." She looked up surprised at hearing a voice.

DeShawn straddled his bicycle at the end of the driveway. "Need some help with that?" he asked.

"Are you serious? I'd love some. I'm sure I have an extra rag for you." She smiled at the boy with the happy eyes.

His warm greeting and offer to help were evidence the teen-ager had made a lot of progress since moving in with his foster parents a year ago. The pastor remembered the first meeting after DeShawn was placed with Russell and Viola Johnson. It was about nine months ago, just shortly after Christine had taken the appointment to the church, when she first approached DeShawn at the weekly Wednesday night dinner. He was helping the men clear the tables after the meal for the church members, collecting the salt and pepper shakers and placing them in a box. She'd made her way over to the gangly teen-ager.

"Hi DeShawn. It's nice to meet you. Thank you for helping this evening."

The handsome boy with cocoa skin had darted his eyes toward the pastor and smiled but hadn't replied, just continued packing up the shakers focusing on his job with his head down.

"Well, I'm glad you're here tonight. You're doing a great job."

"Oh, yeah. I like it here." Christin had to strain to hear his soft voice. He wiped the table off with a cloth smelling of soapy bleach water.

"I'm happy to hear that. You know if you need anything, whether it's a ride to school or any homework help, let me know. Except I should tell you now, I'm not that great in math." Christine had waited for DeShawn to respond so she could give him a wink about the math joke.

The boy's cheek muscles worked. He'd never glanced up toward Christine, just kept wiping the table. "I'll be glad to help you anyway I can," Christine had added with a more serious tone in her voice.

"Uh-huh," he murmured.

Living in the loving foster parents' home allowed DeShawn to blossom and grow into a more confident boy able to trust people who cared about him. Christine watched him become more comfortable with the church family, taking part in the youth group activities, and passing out church bulletins on Sunday mornings. His shy demeanor had been replaced with active participation and conversation with the youth in the church.

Yes, he had come a long way from that scared, shy boy earlier to this helpful young man today. *There's a lot of love and patience in the Johnsons' home.* Christine grabbed another rag for DeShawn and pointed to the bucket of sudsy water. "Knock yourself out."

They worked together easily, washing and rinsing the car, threatening each other with a spraying from the hose, and then drying and polishing the vehicle so it sparkled.

After they finished, Christine stood back to take a look. "Hey, this looks pretty good. What do you say? Do you want a cola or root beer before we tackle detailing the inside of the car?"

Under the shade of the oak tree, she twisted the tab off the pop can and relaxed in the lawn chair next to DeShawn. The cold, refreshing fizz rejuvenated her.

"You can't beat a cold root beer on a warm day. Now if only I had some ice cream to plunk in it for a float." Christine turned to DeShawn for his agreement or protest. Instead he ignored her and stared at the green grass between his sneakers. She waited.

"I been thinkin' about it for a while. I didn't want to say nothin' at first 'cause I didn't want to get in trouble with Mama Johnson for forgetting my jacket at the church that night." He didn't look up.

"Do you mean the night the music director died, DeShawn?" Christine tried to act casual about the possibility of hearing what DeShawn might have seen or heard.

"Yeah." He pulled the tab off the can of root beer and stared at it for a minute. Christine remained silent, allowing him to collect his thoughts. "I need to tell you... I have to tell someone I heard loud voices in the church when I went in to get my jacket. People yelling. It scared me, and I ran away." DeShawn turned his face away and glanced up and down the street.

Christine tried to mask her surprise at his revelation. "I can understand that." She wanted to hear more about what he saw, but didn't want to push too hard for fear he'd feel too uncomfortable to continue.

He faced her. "I didn't want to get involved in a fight 'cause they'd take me away from the Johnsons. I just know it." Christine saw the glistening of tears in his eyes. "Now I wish I'd gone in there. I wish I did, Pastor, 'cause maybe Mr. White wouldn't be dead now. Maybe I could've done something." He scrubbed his eyes with his fists.

She heard the pain in his voice. What courage it took for DeShawn to come to tell her about that night. "Don't even think that."

She rose from her chair and squatted beside DeShawn. He covered his face with his hands. She gently touched his shoulder. "You didn't do anything wrong. Coming to tell me is the right thing to do." She patted his shoulder and then returned to her seat. Christine didn't want to pressure him too much, still she wanted, no, she needed, to find out what he witnessed that night.

"Did you recognize any of the voices?" He brushed his hands across his eyes and cheeks, and then shook his head and looked down. "Could you tell how many men were there?"

"It was just one man and a lady arguing with Mr. White, I think." When he looked up, his sad eyes almost broke her heart.

"Did they yell out any names?" Christine knew she was pushing it.

"No, no names." DeShawn shifted in his chair, his face full of sorrow. "You gotta promise me you won't tell nobody I told you, okay?"

"DeShawn, you can trust me. I won't do anything that could get you in trouble." Torn between protecting DeShawn and finding William's killer, Christine knew in her heart she had to persuade DeShawn to talk to his foster parents.

"No one will take you away from the Johnsons if you tell the police. You didn't do anything wrong. In fact, I think you're pretty brave telling me about the incident. Your information could help to find the person who killed Mr. White." His eyes widened in surprise.

"Think about this. I would like to go with you, so we can discuss this situation with Russell and Viola. I know they'll be proud of you for coming to tell me about that night. It takes a lot of guts to speak up." She sat forward in her chair, studying the face of the anguished boy. "You know Jesus is with you, DeShawn. He loves you and is with you all the time. What would He do in your situation?"

Tears spilled down the boy's cheeks. "Well, Pastor, I know what's right. I'm just scared. If I do the right thing, what'll happen to me?"

"You'll have everyone here in this church family on your side. You have your foster parents to support you, and I promise, I'll stay by your side all the way."

Christine moved to the boy and squatted beside him again. "We'll go together with your foster parents and talk with the detective who will listen to you. You can tell him what you know and have faith in him to understand you and not judge you." Christine honestly believed Cole would handle the situation with care. Remembering his caring attitude with the animals and the kindness he showed her in that circumstance, she felt confident he wouldn't jeopardize the trust she and the boy had built over the last months.

"Do you want me to come home with you, so we can talk to Russell and Viola?" She placed her hands over his, and he didn't pull away.

"Okay, I guess so." She stood up, and the boy dashed the back of his hands across his tear-filled eyes.

"Then let's go after we feed the animals.

Do you want to help me?"

DeShawn's eyes lit up. "Is it true you have a pig and a kangaroo here?"

"I'm afraid so. Come on around back, and you can meet them."

She led DeShawn toward the back yard then stopped so quickly, he almost walked into her. "Oh, noooooo." Christine ran toward Abraham's pen. The pig had rooted up the grass inside the pen. When she and the boy approached him, he grunted happily. "No, no, Abraham."

Turning to the wide-eyed boy, she said, "Looks like we're going to have to move Katy to another spot, too. She's grazed the grass down to just the nubbins there. Iola better get out of the hospital soon. These animals are going to ruin the whole yard," she said. DeShawn laughed and bent over the low fence and scratched Abraham's back.

"Go get the hose and hook it up over there. We need to spray Abraham down. We might as well make some mud puddles for him to play in. Maybe that'll keep him busy instead of digging up the yard. That's what the information on the Internet says to do."

Christine looked at the endearing pig's face. "What are we going to do with you? One thing is for sure. You are definitely not coming in the house." She wagged her finger at the lovable creature. "No telling what the ladies group would do to me for that!"

* * *

"Ella, do you have a minute to talk in my office, or are you in the middle of something?" Christine stood in the doorway of the church office balancing books, laptop case, and an apple.

"Oh, sure. I'll be right there." Ella dropped the reading glasses from her nose and let the beaded necklace attached to the glasses catch them.

Over the weekend, Christine decided she would step up her investigation into William's death. She was going to begin with Ella, the woman who had her finger on the pulse of the church flock.

She sorted out her belongings on the desk and library shelves, giving her some time to think before Ella came in. The secretary had served three pastors in her eleven years as the "right-hand man" to each of them, with knowledge of the workings of the church that only she and the previous pastors discussed. Christine was positive the secretary would have some insight on William and his relationships. She wanted to tap this valuable resource.

The secretary rapped lightly at the open door and stepped into the office. She wore a hot pink blouse, tailored black slacks, and silver circle earrings. Always prepared, Ella was ready with her notebook and pen in her hand.

"Come on in, Ella. Have a seat." She motioned her over to the chair in front of her desk as she settled in her leather desk chair.

"Well, I'll get right down to it. Someone told me on the night of William's murder, there was a lot of yelling going on. What have you heard? Has anyone reported hearing loud voices?" She waited for Ella's response.

Ella creased her forehead. "Who told you that? I've heard a lot of stories, but I can't believe every one of them."

"Did you tell them to the police?"

"The ones I knew at the time, I did. Now, the stories have grown and gotten exaggerated so much, it's hard to sort out the truth from fiction. I haven't said anything more." She fumbled with her notebook and pen in her lap.

"Well, let's go through what you've heard no matter how ridiculous and unbelievable they are. We need to put closure to this investigation and for this congregation to move on. Now, please, tell me everything from the plausible to the most outrageous."

Chapter Seventeen

Late in the afternoon, the long day behind her, Christine walked across the street to the parsonage to check on the animals in the back yard. Her worries seemed to lighten as she rounded the corner of the house and saw Katy and Abraham.

She patted the kangaroo's head. How could this little creature become so precious to her in such a short time? Then there was Abraham. He was too smart for his own good, figuring out how to get under the fence, digging up the yard and plants.

"Pastor Christine." Christine turned her face in the direction of the shout from the side yard. The butterflies in her stomach kicked up. It was Mrs. Arnold Jewell. This woman always stirred up trouble for her. She was making her way alongside the house, slightly bent over her cane. She walked with purpose, although the tight gray curls on her head moved nary a bit. Mrs. Jewell, Christine never felt comfortable enough to call her Florence, was the President of the Ladies Society and had been since Noah set sail on the ark. She wore navy blue slacks with a stylish white shirt. Billboard size navy and gold clip-on earrings flopped from her ear lobes as she shuffled along.

"Hello, Mrs. Jewell. How are you?" She made a quick evaluation of the housekeeping inside the parsonage. Thank goodness the bedroom was upstairs, although she wouldn't put it past the president to sneak up to take a look. She remembered the crumb-covered plate for toast, the buttery knife, and coffee cup from the morning were still on the counter, not in the dishwasher. She rolled her eyes thankful she hadn't been home until this late afternoon to make any more mess in the kitchen or the house.

Recalling the disapproving look she received when Mrs. Jewell discovered she had the cat in the parsonage, she strode toward the old woman to cut her off from viewing the backyard make-shift home for the kangaroo and pig.

"Isn't this a beautiful evening?" The woman was on a mission and unstoppable. Ignoring the question, she detoured around Christine and stopped dead in her tracks when she spotted the animals.

"I couldn't believe it until I saw it with my own eyes. Hazel told me about your having exotic animals plowing up the back yard of the parsonage. This is a disgrace! Just look at this!" She waved her cane to encompass the entire rear area of the property blemished by mud puddles, deep ruts, uprooted bushes, and whole sections of missing grass.

With eyes blazing, she glared at Christine. "You have turned the parsonage yard into a pig pen!"

"Oh, Mrs. Jewell, this is only temporary. I hope you don't think I'm going to keep these animals here. As soon as the animals' owner gets out of the hospital and can travel home, the animals will go with her." She almost said and her gentleman friend, but stopped short, knowing if Mrs. Jewell discovered Iola and Harley were not married and living together, there would be more recriminations and scolding.

"I assure you I will restore the back yard to its former beauty—"

Mrs. Jewell interrupted and shook her index finger at Christine. "I am going to take this up with the Parsonage Committee and the Staff-Parish Committee. I'm surprised no one has stopped this. I'm also going to bring up the fact you have a cat living in my, uh, the church's house. Cat urine can ruin a carpet and the sub-floor, for Heaven's sake." The old woman leaned heavily on her cane. Her face flushed bright scarlet.

Christine wouldn't allow anyone to talk to her like this. Anger reddened her cheeks. She bit her tongue, counted to ten, and then locked eyes with the woman. Her mind raced, searching for a way to handle this situation. She had to calm down and think before saying anything rash.

"Let's go around to the front porch and sit a minute to discuss this." When the pastor swept her hand toward the front of the house, Abraham's happy grunting noises echoed in her ears. Christine turned toward the sounds.

"Abraham," Christine yelled. She spotted him just pulling himself under the fence and blindly trotting over toward the women in his path. When she motioned to stop the little pig, it dawned on her Abraham couldn't see her anyway. So she shouted at him again. Too late. In his joy and exhilaration at being free, he picked up speed and raced toward Christine. He clipped Mrs. Jewell's cane, and the old lady crashed sideways on the green grass.

"Help me, help me," she shrieked, as she lay sprawled on the grass. "That pig is going to eat me." She covered her gray curls with her arms and pulled herself into a ball.

Christine moved at lightning speed to rescue the woman from Abraham's curious nudges. She dragged him away from the frightened woman. "Oh, I am so sorry." She grasped Abraham's halter tightly and tried to help Mrs. Jewell up on her feet with her free hand.

"Are you all right?" Still clutching Abraham, Christine recovered the cane from the lawn and returned it to the disheveled woman.

"Get that creature away from me!" She brushed off her grass-stained white blouse and dark slacks.

Christine tried to help, but Mrs. Jewell slapped her hands away.

In a voice an octave higher than usual, Mrs. Jewell announced, "That animal is a nuisance. I'm calling the Police, Animal Control, and the Church Committees." She limped away, spluttering under her breath and patting what Christine thought were unmovable gray curls back into place.

Christine shook her head as she eyed Abraham who stood calmly at her feet. She attached the leash to the harness and tied it to a small maple tree. "That'll probably be dug up before the night is over. Abraham, Abraham. When is your mother going to come back and claim you?" She couldn't resist scratching the little guy between his ears.

"All right, I'll be back with an apple. I'm not rewarding you with a treat because you knocked old Mrs. Jewell down. I just think you need an apple." Her eyes twinkled with mischief as she headed for the kitchen door.

* * *

Christine filled her cereal bowl with her favorite sweetened cereal flakes and poured lots of cold milk over the top. Just as she picked up her spoon to enjoy her supper, a car pulled into the driveway and stopped. *Probably Mrs. Jewell back with the police now.*

A strong knock at the kitchen door surprised her. She figured police officers would use the front door.

"Christine. It's me." She caught her breath when she opened the door to discover Cole. The black T-shirt molded to his body stretched over every muscle in his broad chest and wide shoulders. She wanted to caress the back of his neck and pull him into her arms.

"Hey, Cole. Come on in. It's good to see you." Her cheeks flushed with heat and she kept her eyes down to have a moment to cool off.

"Well, you may not want to see me under these circumstances." He stepped into the kitchen. "I'm here because we had a report of a killer pig on the premises." His stern eyes and unsmiling face sent her into waves of laughter. Her chuckling was contagious. Cole's sober face broke into a radiant smile. She fell into him, and he put his arms around her. His warm breath on her neck gave her shivers all through her body. She wriggled deeper against his chest. It felt so good. It felt so right.

She kissed him lightly on his lips and then waited for his reaction.

"Hey, don't stop now." He drew her closer with his strong arms, and they stood in the doorway sharing a deep kiss. Heat sizzled through her body. His next kiss urged her lips apart to explore her mouth with quick flicks of his tongue. Dazzling lights showered behind her closed eyes.

Surprised at her intense feelings, she reluctantly stepped back.

"Um, that was nice," he said in a hoarse voice.

"Very nice." She beamed at him. "Maybe you should come and investigate killer pigs here more often."

His smile filled her heart. She hadn't realized it was so empty until now.

Chapter Eighteen

"So how is Iola? Is she out of the hospital yet?" Cole settled into the wooden chair at the small kitchen table. He'd refused Christine's offer of a bowl of cereal but did take her up on a root beer.

"She's out of the hospital and staying at the Up North Motel till her next doctor appointment in a few days. The community service agency is helping Harley with expenses and getting their lives in order." She poured the root beer into the tall glass and set it in front of him. She couldn't take her eyes off of him as he brought the drink to his lips and swallowed the sweet refreshment. Just like his hugs and kisses, very sweet.

She cleared her throat and said, "Harley has access to his bank account now, so I'm going to take him car shopping. He's going to need a big one, probably another van, to take these animals back home."

"I don't think you have to worry too much about the animal control coming after you. I'll talk to the guys and explain this is just a temporary situation."

"It has to be temporary. I'm tired of filling in the holes Abraham's dug out from under the fence. That pig is just too smart. He's been working on opening the gate, too. I'm afraid I'll find him in the neighbors' newly planted gardens anytime now." She frowned.

She took another bite of the sugary flakes of cereal. What more could she want? A bowl of her favorite cereal, cold milk, and a handsome man sitting with her at the table. She shot a quick silent prayer to Heaven saying thank you.

"Is there any information on William's murder?" She tried to ask nonchalantly, so it was not so obvious she was fishing for tidbits about the investigation.

"All the evidence suggests he was definitely hit on the head from behind then broke his neck on the fall down the steps. The time of death had to be between ten p.m. and two a.m. So far, no murder weapon has surfaced and no witnesses." Cole tipped the glass to drain the last drops of the root beer.

"What kind of weapon? Big, little? Where have you looked for it? So the hit on the head killed him, or did the fall kill him?" Her mind was whirling with questions. If only she could get some answers.

"Hold on." He held his palms up as if he were a traffic cop trying to stop the onslaught of vehicles. "I can't tell you anything else. I shouldn't have let this all slip out. I'll be in big trouble if any of this leaks out and they trace it back to me. After all, you're still a person of interest, you know."

Christine was thunderstruck. "Me? Oh, come on—"

Cole stood up and shrugged his shoulders.

"Sorry, I can't say anymore." He made his way toward the kitchen door.

"Cole. You cannot believe I killed William White." With hands on her hips, she stared at him as he opened the door and turned to face her.

"I'm a detective. That's what I do. I'm not a judge. I'm an investigator. I have to find out the truth by getting the evidence. That's all I can say." He disappeared through the doorway into the garage.

No wink, no wave. She knew now he was the one doing the fishing. Trying to catch her as the killer.

Chapter Nineteen

"Chris, I'm re-thinking the idea of sitting here in the basement waiting for the guy who blew through the door and knocked me down last week." Lacey spoke quietly in the church basement bathroom. "I don't think the guy is gonna show up. We've been sitting here for two hours." She held the baseball bat by her side.

Christine switched on the flashlight for a second to check her wristwatch. "Well, let's give him half an hour at least. I don't want to give up too soon. He was here last week at this time. Remember? I told you Cole said he still has me on the suspect list. I've got to talk to this guy. What if he was in the church the night William was murdered? I'd hate to have to come back next week again and wait."

"Oh, wait a minute." Lacey's palm shot up in the air. "You'll have to come back by yourself next week. My nerves can't handle this. Besides what if this is the man who killed William?" Lacey fidgeted with the baseball bat. "I don't think I signed up to catch a murderer when I became your friend."

"Yeah, I owe you one for this, Lacey." Christine hugged her. "Thank you so much for—" She heard the whirr of the elevator. Someone was on the way down to the basement.

Her heart pulsed in her throat.

"All right now, remember when he gets out of the elevator, you turn on the lights, and we trap him. Okay?" The two women rushed to the elevator as the doors opened.

A figure stepped out into the dark hallway. "*Now*, Lacey!" The lights blazed on, and Christine threw her casting net over the surprised man. Not the best cast she had ever thrown, but it fell over the short man and caught him off guard.

"What the hell?" he shouted. He fought the net and jerked at the webbing. Thank goodness the strong fibers wouldn't tear.

Christine hung on to the besieged intruder. Lacey grabbed and yanked the netting around the thrashing man but succeeded only in wrapping the man and herself up in the twists of strong fibers. The two tumbled to the floor thrashing about like fish caught in the net. Christine managed to hang on to him while Lacey figured her way out of the tangle and jumped up. The women bound the net around him as tightly as if he were a newborn baby in a receiving blanket.

"Stop, stop. Stay right there if you know what's good for ya'," Lacey yelled. "We aren't here to hurt you. We just want some answers."

The exhausted trespasser stopped struggling. Christine and Lacey stepped away from him. Lacey recovered her baseball bat and stood over the restrained man, ready to wallop him if he tried to attack them.

"Uh, Lacey, put down the bat. We don't want to scare this guy to death."

Lacey lowered the bat a little, grasping it firmly if needed.

Christine faced the man. "What are you doing in the church at this time of night? What are you after?" She faked a bravado that she hoped was convincing. Her knees felt like gelatin.

"Nothin'. Not doin' nothin'." His dark eyes darted back and forth between both women at warp speed.

"Do you want us to call the cops? Tell us what you're after, or I swear I'll call the police, and you'll be arrested."

"S-s-sorry, miss. I'm sorry." His voice was soft and whiny.

"Tell us why you're here. What are you doing here at this time of night?" Christine demanded.

"I just came to get some food." He sounded like he was going to cry.

"Oh, sure," said Lacey. "The kitchen is closed this time of night."

He stuck out his chin. "Yeah, but the food pantry's open. See, I brung my bags to fill up."

Lacey checked Christine. "Yes, he's right about that. The pantry's never locked."

As the two women looked closer, they could see the man's plastic grocery bags trapped in the netting.

"Are you kidding me? You don't even know where the food pantry is." Lacey spit out the words.

"Yes, ma'am, I do. It's in that big closet, right down this hall and to the right. I need peanut butter and crackers and maybe some beans. Please, let me go. I'm not doin' nothin'. My leg is killin' me."

Christine noticed how his leg was twisted under him as he lay on the floor. The guy was a slight man. She realized she was bigger and stronger than him, especially in this condition. "I'm going to help him up. Okay with you?"

Lacey nodded her head, not taking her eyes off the stranger.

"Okay. You can stand. Don't run. I'm going to get this net off you. We need to talk." Christine carefully removed the net while Lacey brandished the ball bat. She glanced at her friend, seeing a look on Lacey's face that even scared her.

The man awkwardly stood up rubbing his knee and leg. Sprigs of salt and pepper hair sprouted out under a dark knit stocking cap. His denim jacket and faded jeans were in dire need of a thorough cleaning. He scooped up all the plastic bags on the floor holding them tightly to his body.

As Christine watched him pick up the bags, she realized their plan to catch the culprit was good, but they never made plans for what to do with him after they caught him tonight.

"Go ahead to that dining area and sit at the table," Lacey ordered.

The light from the hallway illuminated one

end of the fellowship hall. Christine did not want to turn on all the lights for fear of announcing to the world they were in the basement. She had a feeling this discussion should remain private. She and Lacey stood over the seated, trembling man.

"What's your name?" Christine thought that was a good way to start the interrogation.

"J.R." He sat hunkered down over the table with his bundle of plastic bags spread out before him.

"What's your full name?"

He shrugged his shoulders. "Everybody calls me J. R."

Christine doubted she would get a straight story from the homeless man. J.R. probably wasn't his real name. "How did you get in here? All the doors are locked."

"Oh, I don't use a door, ma'am. I keep a window unlocked and just slip in at night. I sleep down here some nights when it's cold." His eyes seemed sincere to Christine.

She and Lacey exchanged looks. No one ever reported an opened window or that anyone used the church as a shelter. Nothing was ever disturbed.

"Why do you sneak in here at night? Why don't you come when the food is distributed every week? You know you can take all you need for free." Lacey loosened her grip on the ball bat.

"It's kinda hard to find a way to get here when they're open, but I can get a ride on

Wednesday or Thursday nights usually." He bobbed his head as he talked. "Anyway, I don't need much. I only take what I can eat. I don't have no place to store it." He dropped his head and stared at the top of the table. Christine could see how nervous he was as he kept bouncing one knee under the table.

"J.R., I can find you a place to stay every night and food to eat, too. Would you like that?" After working with the community's human service agencies, Christine was familiar with people like J.R who lived in the woods all around the county. Sometimes they stayed with friends or relatives for a while until they wore out their welcome. Then they just made do till the next relative or friend was willing to take them in for a short time. They were the unseen homeless.

J.R.s' eyes brimmed with tears. "I would be so grateful if you could help me, ma'am. I need help real bad." He choked back a sob. "I'm sick, so sick." He pressed his hand to his forehead as if he could push away a headache.

"Okay, J.R. Done. You'll be in a home this evening. I promise." Christine smiled. It was times like this she was thankful for the kind and generous group of people in the church who offered this assistance to people in need any time of day or night. It would only take one phone call to make arrangements.

"A couple of weeks ago, a man died in this basement." Christine watched J.R. for his reaction.

"I didn't do it. I didn't touch him." Both of the amateur detectives jumped at his outburst.

"Did you see who did it?" Lacey moved closer to the suspect.

He shook his head violently. "No, I didn't see him." His eyes darted back and forth to each woman.

"Um, J.R., I think you did see a man here." Lacey stepped toward the man.

"No, ma'am, I didn't see them…" He clasped his hand to his mouth.

"So was there more than just one man, then?" Lacey continued the interrogation.

"Can you describe the others?"

"Wait a minute, lady. You're fixin' to find me a place tonight, and it's gonna be the jailhouse, ain't it?" Anger flashed through his eyes.

"No, J.R. You won't be in jail tonight." She lowered her voice hoping to calm him down. "However, you'll have to talk to the police tomorrow and tell them who you saw here that night."

"Well, I don't know who it was that threw the guy down the steps, but it was a man's voice. Mad, mad as hell at him. I heard the guy yelling 'you can't tell them,' so I got out of here fast when I heard the ruckus."

"What ruckus?"

"When he came fallin' down them stairs over there." Christine and Lacey looked toward the area where J.R. pointed.

He took that second to spring up, throw the

plastic bags at Christine, push Lacey down, and make his break to freedom.

"Hey! Come back here." Christine shouted at the fleeing man. Instead of chasing him, she pulled Lacey to her feet. Lacey held her wrist and spewed a line of blue words Christine had no idea she knew.

"Call the police! Hurry, he's getting away," Lacey yelled.

Christine ran for the phone in the kitchen, picked up the handset from the cradle, then replaced it. She shook her head and picked it up again, listened for the dial tone, and again returned it to the cradle. What would she tell them? A homeless man just escaped from her after she'd grilled the guy about murdering someone? The sick old guy didn't need any more problems piled up on him.

Grabbing some ice from the freezer in the kitchen, she wrapped it in a kitchen towel on her way out and offered it to Lacey. "Here, put this ice on your wrist. Let's go back to my house."

Christine held out the icy towel to her injured friend. As Lacey pressed the ice to her wrist, she asked, "You didn't call the police, did you?"

"Um, no. The line was dead." Christine said a quick prayer for forgiveness for the lie.

Chapter Twenty

The next morning Christine heard the knock on her office door. She was expecting Harry Perkins, President of the Board, to arrive for a discussion. She didn't relish the idea of defending herself to Harry and to the board about keeping Katy and Abraham in the parsonage yard. She pasted a welcoming smile on her face and opened the door.

"Hello, Harry, all decked out for golf, I see." He wore his usual plaid shirt paired with aqua blue shorts. Christine grasped his hand in a warm handshake. "Have a seat. What a gorgeous day for golf!"

"Yes, it is, and today I think I'm actually going to get out there and hit a hole-in-one." The doctor, supposedly retired, always seemed to have some other project to keep him from his beloved golf game.

She eased into her desk chair while the president settled into the chair across from her. She saw the twinkle in his eyes fade and his mouth turn down. She braced herself for the inquisition on Mrs. Jewell's visit.

"I suppose you talked with Mrs. Jewell about the incident yesterday at the parsonage. I understand why she—"

"No, well, yes, I did talk with her," Harry

interrupted, "and listened to her usual complaints. That's not why I'm here."

Christine squelched a sigh of relief. Mrs. Jewell must have a reputation for stirring up trouble, she surmised.

"Jim Long, you know he's the Chairman of the Church Finance Committee, came to me with some concerns about financial irregularities found in the latest unscheduled audit."

Christine stiffened in her chair. "What do you mean?"

"There's about ten thousand dollars missing. It can't be accounted for in our records and bank statements. It has simply disappeared."

She could not stop the surprised gasp from escaping her lips. She sat up straight in her chair and waited for Harry to laugh and say it was just a joke, but no grin etched across his face.

He continued. "Once in a while, the auditor takes a look at the books during the year checking things out as well as auditing at the beginning of the year. After we discovered the error last week, Jim and the treasurer, Mason O'Leary, and I have quietly been checking out the procedures, the accounts, the bank statements, statements of giving. You name it. We didn't want to bring this up until we knew for sure there was a real problem."

"So you believe it is a real problem," she asked.

Harry nodded. "I'm afraid so. We need to talk to every person who has access to the money—the ushers, counters, board officers, finance committee members, and the staff members, including you." He glanced down at his hands folded in his lap. "I'm sorry, Pastor. I hate to burden you with this on top of the investigation into William's death, but we really shouldn't wait any longer." Christine heard the urgency in his voice. "We need to start the interviews right away. If nothing is found, then we'll need to take it to the next step."

"What's that?" Christine dreaded to hear it.

He placed his palms on the desk. "We'll notify the police. Instead of a simple error in bookkeeping, or a deposit to the incorrect account, it would be likely that someone is stealing the church's money."

Christine held her palm up to stop Harry. "Oh, I understand how badly you want to find out what has happened. Let's not jump to any conclusions. Let's just take it one step at a time. I want to go over everything with you, Jim, and Mason. We need to keep this as quiet as possible. I don't need to tell you our church is very fragile now."

After setting up a plan of action with Harry, they shook hands and she closed the door behind him. With her back against the door, Christine closed her eyes and took a deep breath. She prayed for Jim, Mason, Harry, and herself to grant them the expertise to discover the reason for the missing money and for strength and wisdom to help guide her through this next hurdle.

After her amen, her eyes popped open with the realization—she was not only a murder suspect, she was accused of being a thief, too.

Chapter Twenty-One

Christine had a hard time processing Harry's account of the missing church money. The thought someone would steal from the church was impossible for her to accept.

A rap at the office door a few minutes later interrupted her thoughts on how to proceed with the internal investigation. Knowing she had to assume her pastoral personality, she brushed her bangs from her forehead and answered, "Come in. I'm here."

"Got a minute, Pastor?" Cole's face appeared around the slightly opened door. Christine couldn't keep her mouth from turning up at the corners or calm her thumping heart. He seemed to be shielding his body from her behind the wooden door. Was he afraid she was going to throw rotten tomatoes at him because of the last meeting?

"Yes, I do, Cole. Come on in."

He eased himself into the chair in front of her desk. He was dressed smartly in his chinos, navy blue shirt, and tie. She assumed this was an official visit from the detective. No social call. She wished he were calling on her as a friend, maybe even more than a friend.

"Are you coming to visit me as a suspect in the case or just for a chat?" She straightened her back in the chair, flipping her pen on the desk.

"A person of interest." Her eyes opened wide, but before she could comment, Cole said, "I've never said you are a suspect."

"I think that's a question of semantics." She held both hands out in front of her, palms upward like a Scales of Justice. She raised the right palm. "Suspect," she said, and lowered the right palm. "Or person of interest." She raised her left palm. "They both mean the same thing. You're still trying to prove I murdered William."

"Hear me out, please." Cole edged forward on his chair. "I'm here to apologize." She heard the sincerity in his voice and could feel the warmth in his eyes. "I'm sorry if I upset you. I was just as angry with myself as you were with me. I'm having a hard time separating my professional role from my personal feelings for you."

She shifted in her chair, wishing the desk was not between them. What could she say to this wonderful man? "Well, I really like you, Cole." She felt like she was back in seventh grade telling her boyfriend, not a grown man. She bit her lip wondering how to admit to him she had feelings for him too. "Only people whom I care about can hurt me so deeply. I don't want you to believe I could murder William."

"Please, let's start over. I have to keep investigating this case. We're a small police department. I have to do the job. I can't let my feelings for you cloud my objectivity. Can you accept that?"

She took in the sincere expression on his face, his dark brown eyes. Pressing her hand against her stomach to stop the butterflies circling in there, she replied, "Yes, I can understand your position. If only I could prove to you..."

"That's why I'm here. I have the proof to dismiss you as a person of interest."

She saw the sparkle in his eyes and sat back in her leather chair breathing a sigh of relief. "At last. But what? What proved it to you?"

"We have your cell phone records. You made several calls, including to your parents, that evening during the time of the murder. I don't think you'd be fighting with William and whacking him on the head while talking to your parents." His smile lit up her heart.

She wanted to jump over the desk and hug him. "Would it be improper if I came around the desk and gave the detective a big hug for his fantastic detective work?"

He stood up, and before he could answer, she was out of her chair and in his arms.

"Well, I must say, I've never had anyone show me that much appreciation when I told them they'd been cleared." His light chuckle filled her soul.

She hated to move away from his embrace. It felt so right being in his arms, but she pulled away from him to resume her role as Pastor Christine.

"All right now. Sit down please. I need to

talk to you." She waved her hand toward the chair and watched him take the seat.

"How about going for coffee?" he asked as she settled into her desk chair.

She glanced at her wristwatch. "I would love to after I tell you some important things you need to know about the investigation."

Cole's eyes narrowed. "What do you mean?"

Christine breathed in deeply before she could begin. "I just spoke with Harry Perkins, the board president." She tried to wrap her mind around what she was about to say. "He implied someone could be stealing money from the church funds."

The detective whistled softly. "How much is missing?"

Christine mumbled, "Ten thousand dollars." She didn't like the look on the his face. "They—"

Cole interrupted. "Who's they?"

"Jim Long, Chairman of the Church Finance Committee, and Mason O'Leary, our treasurer, are working with Harry. Going over the books, procedures."

Cole nodded his head. "Our forensic accounting officers could find discrepancies quickly and preserve the evidence for prosecution."

"Wait, Cole. We decided not to bring the police into this until we check every record and after we talk with all the people who handle the money and have access to the accounts. There has got to be a mistake. A number transposition, a dropped decimal…"

"Ten thousand dollars is quite, as you say, a large mistake." He shook his head.

"Please, wait, and let me finish. I only requested some time to turn it into the police because we've been so battered by the police investigation into William's death. We need to keep it within the church group who would be accountable for the funds and spending. Then we'll turn everything over to the police with all the information we've discovered." She stopped to gather her thoughts.

"What if it *is* just an error, an incorrect entry into the wrong fund? We can't jump to judgment until we have all the facts. Can you understand that?" Her eyes pleaded as she defended her position.

"Believe me. I do understand where you're coming from. I'm a cop. I think like a cop." Cole averted his eyes for a second then looked at Christine. "This may have something to do with William's murder."

Christine was speechless. She searched his eyes and saw the earnestness in them. She realized this could be the key to the murder investigation. "All right then. Will you give us some time to check a few more things before we turn this over to the police?"

"Christine, I'll work quietly with Harry Perkins. He and the committee can take the lead on the questioning."

She sighed. Actually it was a relief to know

Cole was there to help them. "Okay. I'll give you his phone number, so you can all meet together." She retrieved the tattered church member directory she always kept on her desk to look up the phone number.

"Sounds good." His deep brown eyes softened. "I hope you realize how much I do care about your church congregation, but we need to check out everything, no matter how inconsequential it may seem."

Christine's eyes clouded. Was this the time to tell him about J.R.?

"What? What are you thinking, Hobbs? You're keeping something from me, aren't you?" The detective moved forward in his chair.

She didn't like the idea Cole could read her thoughts so easily. "Well...we did have an incident, or maybe you wouldn't call it an incident. I mean... I don't know what you would call it." She pulled a strand of hair behind her ear.

"Just tell me, please." A frown creased his forehead, and impatience tinged his voice as he said, "And who is 'we' anyway?"

"Lacey and I discovered an intruder in the basement the other night. We tried to catch him, and the first time he got away." Her words tumbled from her mouth.

"The first time he got away?" Cole sprang from his chair and paced the room as Christine divulged the entire story.

"Well, yes. Then later we waited for him to appear, and sure enough, we caught him. His name is J. R., a homeless man who was stealing food from the church food pantry." She spoke more rapidly. "I wanted to help him. Get him a place to stay for the night and a decent meal. He told us he sneaks into the church and spends the night here. He was very sorry."

"Oh, sure. Sorry he got caught. You should have called the police." Anger colored his voice. The detective stopped pacing. "You have no idea what could have happened to you, do you? He could be a desperate man using desperate measures to get away from you two naïve girls."

She stood up to face the agitated detective. "Well, he ran away from *us girls*. I guess *we girls* scared him." Holding her hands to her sides with fists tightly clenched, she felt the crimson color her cheeks.

"Well, you were lucky this time. If this is the same J. R. I know, he's mainly a small time robber. Petty theft like stealing leftovers and junk from garbage cans and breaking into cars for loose change, food, and clothes. He's spent more than a few nights in jail for intoxication. Everyone knows him down at the station. I'll make a call and have him brought in." Cole shook his head.

"As long as we're being honest here—" Christine did not want to continue anticipating Cole's reaction. "Before he ran away, we asked him about the night William White was murdered." She stepped toward Cole as she delivered the next bit of information to the detective. "I believe he was in the church that night. He's a witness."

"He was in the church that night? And you are just now telling me?" The detective opened his arms wide. "Do you realize he could be more than a witness, perhaps the killer?"

She couldn't imagine that skinny old guy being a murderer. "Oh, come on, Cole."

"So what other secrets are you keeping from the police, Pastor Hobbs?"

Christine flinched at the sarcastic tone in Cole's voice. "Nothing. That's it. Can't think of another thing." She felt her body flush hot, knowing she was lying to him. She didn't want to reveal the conversation with DeShawn and his foster parents. After supporting the teen while he told them what he witnessed, Christine wanted to accompany the family to the police station to talk to Cole. In fact, they planned to go together after school later that day.

"This afternoon I'll have another possible witness for you to talk to in your office." She stopped him before he could say anything. "I promised him, Cole. I can't tell you anything."

She sensed Cole's suspicious eyes boring into her. "Christine. Don't try to play detective. You could find yourself way in over your head." His eyes locked onto hers. "This is not a game. Let us do the investigating."

She moved close to him. "I know. I know it isn't a game. It's hard to just stand by when people you care about are accused of murder." She gently placed her fingers on his lips as Cole began to speak again. "I'll be careful, and I will definitely inform you of everything I learn from now on." She searched his face. The anger was gone, replaced by concern.

"All right. We'll work together, but you will stay out of harm's way. Do you understand?" He rested his hands on her shoulders, holding her an arm's length away. Christine knew he was waiting for her to agree with his request.

"Okay, Cole. We're a team. Now," she asked quietly, "do you still want to go for coffee?"

He gently pulled her close. She drew in the fragrance of his citrus cologne, the fresh crisp laundry scent from his shirt. Her anxiety and frustration melted away as he held her securely.

"Just one condition," she said as she stepped back. "While we're having coffee, no more talk about the investigation, William, or the missing money…"

"That's a deal. I'll call in to have J. R. picked up. Then we'll go." Pulling his cell phone from his belt, Cole opened the office door wide and escorted her into the hallway. Somehow she felt lighter than she had in a long time.

Chapter Twenty-Two

Christine sat at her kitchen table the next afternoon. The cup of coffee cooled as she recalled everything that had happened the day before. The worst thing was Harry's news about the missing funds. With the sip of coffee, the afternoon visit to the police station with DeShawn and the Johnsons played in her mind. What a relief for DeShawn. She was proud of the young man for being so brave to come forward with what he saw and heard that scary night. He was lucky to have the Johnsons as foster parents, or was that a God-thing, not just a coincidence? They were so supportive and loving.

The best thing about yesterday, yes the very best thing, was the hours she and Cole had spent together. A smile spread across her lips as she recalled their coffee date yesterday morning.

Christine glanced at the old kitchen clock on the wall as she tickled the fur between the cat's ears. "Bitsy, look at the time. I don't have time to daydream today. I have to visit folks at the hospital and get back in time for the planning committee meeting tonight." She dumped the comfortable cat off her lap and rinsed her cup at the kitchen sink.

She glanced out the window to see her secretary scurrying across the parking lot toward the parsonage. Ella's face was twisted into a frightening mask of fear. Christine raced to the garage door, opened it, and yelled to Ella. "I'm here. Come on in."

Ella shot through the doorway. "Mason is on his way to get me."

"What? What do you mean? Come and sit down." She escorted the anxious woman to the kitchen and pulled out a wooden chair from the table.

"I have to get out of here. I must leave now. Can I use your car? He'll surely find me if I drive mine."

"Why, Ella? What happened?"

Ella slumped into the chair and tried to catch her breath.

"Last night after the meeting, Mason came home. He was very agitated. He went to his computer and closed the door. He didn't come out all night. When I was getting ready for work this morning, he was still in there. I tapped on the door to tell him the coffee was ready. He told me he had work to do and to just go away." The tears flowed from Ella's eyes.

Handing Ella a tissue from her pocket, Christine asked, "Did he hurt you, Ella?"

"Oh, no. I just left him alone and left for the church.

"He called just now and said he'd packed our bags. He's supposed to pick me up, and we're going to leave town. I told him I didn't want to leave. He yelled at me, Christine. He cussed at me. He's never acted like this. I'm afraid of him.

Truly afraid he's losing his mind." She twisted the tissue in her hands.

"You have no idea what's up? What he's running away from?"

Ella put her head down and dabbed her eyes and nose with the tissue. "I don't want to stay here. He's scaring me. I surely don't want to go with him. Give me the keys to your car, Pastor. He won't think to look for me in your car. I'll be safe at my sister's in Newport."

Christine frowned. She didn't recall Ella ever talking about her sister, but Ella was desperate for help. Perhaps an estranged sister was the answer for the moment. Ella's safety was the first priority. "Okay. Do you know where he was when he called you? How much time do we have before he arrives?"

"I'm already here."

Christine and Ella turned to see Mason at the open kitchen door. Fear gripped Christine's heart. Looking into Mason's eyes, instead of a delightful little leprechaun, a crazed wild man stared back with his hunting rifle aimed right at her.

Christine caught her breath and stepped away from him. She could not tear her eyes away from the pointed rifle. *Breathe deeply. Stay calm.*

"Mason. Mason! Stop this," Ella screamed. "Put that rifle down now. Please, darling. Please."

Christine moved behind Ella and placed her hands on the shoulders of the trembling woman. She knew she had to keep Mason calm and Ella provoking him only made him more agitated. She had no idea what he could do in this fragile state of mind.

"Mason, please let us know what you need. Whatever you say. We can do it." Christine's soft voice and her re-assuring demeanor seemed to register with the man. "What do you want?"

Mason hobbled over to the counter and leaned on it to hold himself upright pointing the gun down to the floor. He was breathing heavily. Perspiration glistened on his face. Christine noticed he must have left his cane in the car. Where was his car? She didn't hear him drive up to the house.

"I want a glass of water, please." His voice sounded like Mason, but his face was not the congenial countenance of the man she knew.

With slow, deliberate steps, Christine moved to the sink and ran the cold water, then pulled a clean glass from the cupboard. As she filled it with the clear, cool liquid, she silently prayed. *Dear Lord, we need some intervention from you. Help me know how to handle Mason and find a way to keep us safe. I'm listening and open to all ideas. Thank You, Lord."*

She handed the water glass to Mason, who stood only a couple of steps away from the sink. She let him drink several swallows while her heart pounded so hard in her chest she feared both Mason and Ella could hear the thumping. Trying to keep her composure, her mind raced with ideas on how to handle the distraught man. Sure, she was a lot taller and stronger than this man but he had a rifle in his hands.

Christine looked to the ceiling anticipating

some help from Heaven. She inhaled deeply to clear her mind. "Mason, you're upset. Please tell us what's wrong, so we can help you. "She watched Mason's hand holding the water glass shake. "Let's go sit down and talk over whatever is bothering you. Please trust me. You know I love you." She motioned for him to sit at the table.

"It's all right, Mason. I'll go with you now. Don't worry. Everything'll be okay." Ella pushed the kitchen chair back from the table and stood up holding on to the back of the chair as if it could shield her from Mason.

"No, Ella. It isn't going to be okay," he cried out. "Don't you understand? It's not going to be okay!" Christine watched the old man's face flame dark red.

"Mason, there's no need to involve Pastor Christine. She isn't going to hurt you." As Ella moved closer to Mason, Christine reached for her large leather bag stashed near the toaster on the counter. She fumbled around for her phone.

"You know she'll call the cops before we can get away. We can't have her call the cops." The man's eyes brimmed with tears as he whined to his beloved. Mason turned toward Christine. His eyes narrowed when he saw the pastor's back to him. "Turn around, Christine. Turn around now," he demanded, pointing the rifle at her back. "Stop it. Stop it." His anger twisted his face into an unrecognizable image of Mason.

Christine whirled around, glancing directly at the rifle. "I'm getting my phone," she said in a quiet voice as she pulled it from her bag. "I'll call the police, Mason, or you can put the rifle down, and we can talk." She flipped the phone open and hit the speed dial button for 9-1-1. "Just put the rifle down and talk, Mason. Please."

"Nooooooooooo…" Mason lunged and struck her arm with the rifle. The cell phone skittered across the linoleum floor under the kitchen table, coming to a halt as it bumped into the leg of the table.

The pain from the blow of the rifle exploded up her arm. Christine grabbed her arm and clenched her teeth to keep from crying out. At least it wasn't broken. She could wiggle her fingers, but she'd have a colorful bruise there. She felt a lump already beginning to form and the heat rush into the area on her forearm.

She reminded herself to stay calm, although at this moment she was ready to go ballistic. Biting her lip to keep from yelling at Mason, she studied his distorted features and his manic eyes. This was not the sweet man she knew. Some demon had taken over his body.

"That's enough. We're all leaving now! Get out, both of you!" He waved the rifle toward the door. "Get in the pastor's car now. We're going to Mexico." The man's loud voice split the air.

Mason grabbed the kitchen countertop with one hand for support. Keeping the rifle aimed at the two women with the other, he waited for Ella and Christine to pass by him before he followed them out through the kitchen door into the garage.

She recalled the advice from police when in this situation. Don't allow yourself to be taken to a different location. As she trudged out the kitchen door and into the garage, she knew she had to act now or else.

Something flashed into Christine's vision. She heard familiar squeals and looked behind her to witness Abraham racing through the back door of the garage. Before she could react to spotting the pig, he crashed into Mason, upending the tottering old man. The rifle flew up in the air, and Mason landed hard on the concrete garage floor. Abraham snorted and prodded the prone man.

"Get him away. Get him away from me!" Mason screamed. The pig kept poking and slobbering all over Mason, as he lay helpless on the garage floor.

Christine kicked the rifle away from Mason.

"Ella, quick get my phone and call--" She stopped when she heard the police sirens out front.

Ella hurried to the side door of the garage and opened it. She waved at the cruisers and shouted, "We're in here."

Chapter Twenty-Three

Ella frantically motioned the uniformed officers into the garage. Christine felt as if the cavalry arrived. She needed to sit down. Her knees shook so hard she thought she might collapse. It was ridiculous to feel so frightened because she was safe now, but evidently her knees hadn't gotten the message.

Thank You, Lord. Thank You for sending Abraham to the rescue. He's a unique hero. You are always full of surprises for me.

Watching the officers trying to avoid ardent Abraham to get to Mason made her grin. What a great pig. Gathering her strength, Christine hustled over to protect Abraham from the officers, or was it the other way around?

"Need some help with Abraham?" She heard Cole's voice behind her. Turning to see him join the two officers, he grabbed the halter and pulled the excited pig away from Mason. One officer immediately handcuffed the crying man while he lay on the floor.

Bending down over Abraham, Cole spoke quietly and petted the hero pig. Abraham responded to the calming familiar touch. Grabbing the pig by his harness, he escorted the animal away to the back of the garage and asked an officer to take him back to the pen and make sure he couldn't get out again.

Ella tried to get near Mason, but the officers wouldn't allow it. A female officer shuffled Ella into the kitchen away from the scene.

When the wailing ambulance siren announced its arrival in the parsonage driveway, Cole joined the officers. "How is he?"

"He's pretty shook up, and his leg's in bad shape," a uniformed policeman replied. "We're waiting for the EMTs to check him out. He's babbling on about being sorry."

"Get him in the ambulance and transport him to the hospital. Stand guard. We're taking him into custody. No one talks to him till I get there."

Cole moved close to Christine. "Oh, Cole, am I ever happy to see you guys." She realized she was gushing but couldn't hold back the relief she felt to be free from Mason.

"Are you hurt?" His hands moved to her arms and peered into her eyes.

Emotion flooded over her and she couldn't stop her body from trembling. Tears glided down her cheeks. "I'm fine. I need to check on Ella." She pulled a tissue from her pocket as she entered the kitchen from the garage.

"You sure you're okay?" His concern for her warmed her heart. She couldn't speak with so much emotion coursing through her mind and body. She only nodded.

Cole took her arm and escorted her to the kitchen door. "I'll be there in a minute when I finish up out here." He squeezed her arm and watched as stepped into the kitchen.

"Ella, oh, Ella." Christine bent down and embraced the anguished woman sitting on the kitchen chair. "Are you all right?" Ella sat with her hands in her lap, twisting a wadded tissue, her eyes red-rimmed and face pale.

"This is a nightmare. A nightmare. What just happened? I can't believe that was my Mason. I don't know that monster!" She broke down. Christine hugged her friend again, then sat down beside her.

Ella dabbed at her eyes. "What's going to happen to Mason? What will they do to him?" Her voice faltered, and she hid her face in her hands.

"I'm so sorry, Ella. I don't know what will happen. We'll have to deal with it as it comes. You know we can handle anything with God's help."

Chapter Twenty-Four

Cole entered the kitchen and stood quietly, watching the two women. He was in awe of Christine and her strength to console this woman when she herself had been through the same ordeal. He wanted to go to her and wrap her in his arms. Wishing he didn't have to be the detective for this case, he tried to keep his professional persona intact.

Christine turned toward him. "How in the world did you know? How did you know we needed the police?"

"You dialed 9-1-1, didn't you, for help?"

"Well, I hit the speed dial. I had no idea the call actually went through because Mason knocked the phone out of my hand. An angel must have been listening." The throbbing pain in her injured arm brought back the image of Mason and his crazed eyes. She shuddered.

Ella gently dabbed at her nose with a tissue. "You know he's out of his mind, Detective. He doesn't know what he's saying." Her swollen eyes darted up to meet his. "He isn't acting like himself."

She averted her eyes to the kitchen tabletop. Cole could feel her close herself off from him. He understood her feelings. She would resent him because he would be the bad guy, the one who would question Mason, the one to arrest him for breaking into Christine's home with a rifle, threatening them, and holding them against their will.

Pulling a tissue from the box on the countertop, Cole approached the women. He gently touched Ella's shoulder and handed her the fresh tissue. "Mason will get good care at the hospital. I'm going to talk to the doctors and find out about his condition," he said. "If you want to go to the hospital and wait while I talk to Mason, you can. I have a car outside to take you."

"I can drive her." Christine circled the table to stand by him.

Cole tried to read her eyes, wanted to assure her everything would be okay. Instead, he drew her into him, moulding her body against his. He felt her relax in his embrace. It felt right. He forgot about his role as a detective, thinking only of Christine, and thankful she wasn't harmed by the mad man.

She stepped away from him, wiping her brimming eyes with her fingers. He reached into his back pocket for his clean white handkerchief and handed it to her.

As Christine mopped away her tears, she said, "I'll take Ella to the hospital and sit with her. We can wait there together, can't we, Ella?"

"Um, yes. We can, but I can drive myself. I wonder where Mason left his car."

"We'll find it. However, you can't use it. We'll need to take a look at it," Cole said.

"Fine then, I'll just drive my car over." She stood up and straightened her blouse.

"Are you sure you're okay to drive? This has been pretty tough for you," Cole said.

Ella pulled her shoulders back and faced the detective. "I told you I'm just fine." Turning to Christine, she said, "Let me get my things at the office, and I'll meet you at the hospital."

* * *

Although Ella insisted he didn't need to, Cole walked her to the church. It was a chilly walk, not because of the weather, but because Ella ignored the detective's questions. He wondered if she were in shock, the way her personality changed in front of him. He tried to keep in mind how she would feel. Ella thought of him as the guy who'd be questioning the love of her life and gathering evidence to put him in jail.

Ella finally spoke when they arrived at the Church. "I can go on in to the office and get my things, Detective. I'm quite capable and feeling much better. You can leave now." Then she turned her back to him and ascended the concrete steps, entering the church without looking back.

Assured she was strong enough to go on alone, and very aware she didn't want him around, Cole returned to the parsonage where Mason was ready to be transported to the hospital.

"I'll see you at the hospital, sir," he told the injured man who was strapped onto the stretcher. Mason only sighed and closed his eyes. The EMT slammed the doors, and the heavy vehicle pulled out of the driveway.

Anxious to check on Christine, he strode up the driveway, into the garage, and crossed the kitchen door threshold. "Christine. Christine. Where are you?" No answer. She was gone. His heart throbbed with fear as he raced through the house. "Chris. Chris."

"I'm in here. I'll be out in a minute," she yelled back to him.

Red-faced, he waited outside the bathroom door.

How could a woman wiggle herself into his heart so quickly? He shook his head in disbelief. Nearly losing Christine because of this crazed man jolted him into realizing how precious she had become to him.

Cole felt foolish standing in the hallway by the bathroom, so he moved a few feet away from the door and leaned against the wall, arms crossed in a relaxed gesture. "What's taking so long?" he mumbled under his breath. "Are you okay?" he called down the hall.

"Yeah. Just a second."

Now standing straight, he stretched and dropped his arms to his side. He didn't realize he was tapping his foot impatiently on the hard wood floor.

"Umm, maybe I'd better get going."

"Oh, just a minute. I'm about ready."

He drew closer to the door and heard water running in the lavatory basin. *What the heck, it doesn't take this long to wash your hands.*

The door opened. Christine stood in the doorway, pale and beautiful. Her grin captivated him.

"I'm sorry to keep you waiting. My stomach was a bit upset. I got a little sick. I guess I was more scared and nervous than I thought. A splash of cold water, tooth brushing, and I'm ready for whatever comes next." She laughed in embarrassment.

Cole covered the next three steps in an instant and hugged her tightly. She didn't resist. Instead he could feel her arms tighten around the back of his neck. The current of electricity dazzled him as they embraced.

He stepped back from Christine and noticed the color returning to her glowing face. With a sparkle in her eyes, her mouth turned up into a smile. He surrendered to those lips, kissing her deeply. And miracles of miracles, she kissed him back passionately.

"Well, I feel better, a lot better now." She grinned as she stayed close and focused on his lips.

He returned her good-natured smile. He kissed her again and again. He couldn't resist kissing her eyes, her cheeks, her hair.

Christine finally pulled away. She straightened her suit coat and smoothed her pencil skirt. "I think I'd better get over to the hospital to check on Mason and Ella. She flashed her flirty eyes at Cole. "I'd love to stay here with you, but, um, don't you have to get over there, too?"

Unfortunately, Christine's question nudged him back to the present situation, a cop on a case. The kisses made him forget he was on duty and should be leaving for the hospital to interrogate the perpetrator. Instead he felt his heart pounding and his body flushed with heat, aching to remain in her arms.

"Oh, yeah, I guess we do have to face reality. I need to question Mason, and you need to do whatever you have to do. When we're done, I'll meet you here tonight. Okay?"

"Okay. I'll keep the light on for ya'." Christine laughed and turned her thumbs up.

Cole felt lost again in her eyes. He quickly pecked her on the cheek to break the spell and headed for his car.

Chapter Twenty-Five

Christine scurried to the kitchen to find her bag. Beside it she discovered her cell phone. Someone must have picked it up from the floor and left it for her. A quick check proved the cell phone was still working. *Amazing.* Funny how her arm was all better now. *I guess kisses do help relieve pain.*

As she dropped the phone into her bag, she glanced out the window to see Ella's car in the parking lot. She should have left for the hospital by now.

Christine sprinted up the church steps two at a time and raced into the silent interior, searching for Ella. She ran down the hall toward the church office and grabbed the doorknob. It wouldn't turn. She rattled it and pushed on the door, but it was locked. Christine was puzzled. Ella never locked the office unless she left to go on an errand.

She pounded on the door. "Ella. Are you in there? Are you all right?"

Listening at the door, she thought she heard someone rustling papers. She reached for the keys in her pocket and unlocked the office door. When she swung the door open, Ella stood beside the doorway. A cloth bag straining to contain all of the contents sat on the desk.

"Oh, it's you, Pastor." Ella's voice sounded strained and formal.

"I saw your car still in the lot. I was worried about you. Are you okay?"

Ella stepped back to allow the pastor to enter the office. "Come on in."

Christine's gaze connected with Ella's. Her eyes looked unusually bright. The pastor strode around behind the desk. She spotted several more of Ella's book bags sitting on the floor next to the desk chair. She knew Ella was an avid reader, but these bags were stuffed as if they would burst at the seams.

"My goodness." She smiled. "It looks like you're preparing to stay at the hospital a long time. Your bags are chocked full of books and magazines? Or did you pack a big lunch?" Christine stepped closer to the bags to peer inside.

Ella giggled and moved like she was shooing the pastor away from her. "Oh, never mind. I was just leaving. I'll meet you at the hospital like we planned. Poor Mason. He's going to need you to say a few prayers for him." She fidgeted with her beaded necklace.

Christine scrutinized the cloth bags sitting on the floor, remembering how dedicated Ella was to recycling and living a green life. Christine's eyes narrowed. She reached in and pulled out a manila folder. A church file.

"Please, Christine, you need to get over to see Mason. Go on, please." Ella motioned to the door. Christine glimpsed a thumb drive between

Ella's thumb and forefinger and glanced over at the computer screen. The desktop was up.

"Ella, don't worry about work here. You don't have to finish up. Just head on over to the hospital. I'll turn off your computer." The pastor bent over to shut down the computer, scanning over the programs stored at the bottom of the screen.

"Like I said, I'm ready to go," Ella said in a flat voice. She unzipped her purse sitting on the edge of the desk.

"It looks like you're working on the financial reports." Christine frowned as she studied the screen more closely. "What are you doing with these right now?" She needed an explanation. There were no finance meetings scheduled which would need reports this week. Why would the treasurer ask her for information? Ella had no reason to access these files at this time when she should be at the hospital with Mason.

Her heart beat in her throat. The dull throb of a headache began hammering in her brain. There was no reason for Ella to access the files unless she was changing the reports.

Christine glanced up at Ella, hoping for a reasonable explanation. She froze when she saw Ella pointing a small handgun at Christine's chest.

"What in the world? Ella..." Christine jumped back and stared wide-eyed at the weapon.

"You couldn't just leave it alone, could

you?" Ella hissed. "I didn't want you involved in this, Pastor. I didn't want you to know me like this."

"Involved in what?" Her stomach flipped. She thought she was going to be sick again. "Please, put the gun down, Ella. Let's talk this through." Christine motioned to lay the weapon down on the desk.

"No. I have to leave, and you can't come with me, so I have no choice. As soon as Mason spills his guts about everything, the police will look for me." Christine saw the look of a cornered animal in Ella's eyes.

"Open the desk drawer and get out the duct tape now." Ella braced herself against the desk and extended her arm holding the gun straight out in front of her. Christine could smell the pistol aimed at her face.

"You have a choice. Think about what you're doing." Christine's mind flashed back to the training she had for dealing with a hostage situation, but this time she was the hostage. She stepped toward Ella.

"Stay back." Ella waved the pistol toward Christine. "I don't want to hurt you. I will if I have to." Her voice was as hard as the steel gun she pointed at Christine's head. "I didn't want it to happen like this. You have to believe that. Everything was fine until William figured it out."

"What did William figure out? Tell me what you're talking about." Christine tried to make sense of what Ella was saying. Looking down the barrel of a gun scares concentration away from anything other than the thought of escape. She had to keep focused on Ella, keep her talking until she could work out what to do. *Lord, I'm calling on You once again to help me out of another jam. Please help me. I need You, Lord.* She closed her eyes for a moment and took a quick breath.

"Please, Ella. Let's talk about this. We can find a way together. We're a team, you and me." Christine's eyes darted about the room looking for a way out or a hiding place. Unfortunately, the desk and Ella were between her and the door, and the room was way too small to hide from the threatening secretary. Buying time by talking was her only defense at the moment.

"William was going to tell the police if Mason didn't go and confess to cooking the books as he called it." Ella's eyes gleamed with a sheen of tears. She wiped them away with her gun-free hand. Her voice became low and soft.

"Mason and I figured out how to keep two sets of books for the church." She sighed. "You know Mason is a brilliant CPA. He knew how to do that, and I had access to all the records, so it was easy to juggle the accounts. William began questioning Mason about it. At first, he thought Mason had made a mistake with the bookkeeping. Then he became suspicious." Ella wiggled the gun. "Get the duct tape out of the top desk drawer."

"So you've been playing me for a fool? You just pretended you loved our church and me because you and Mason were getting rich with your deception?" Christine practically spat out the hateful words.

"I got clothes, jewelry, gifts, and stashed some of the cash away. He was so crazy about me he'd buy me anything I wanted." Pride flashed across her face. "I knew it would all have to end sometime. I waited too long. I should've been cut of here after that idiot Mason killed William," Ella snarled.

Christine sucked in her breath, nearly collapsing with the discovery that Mason murdered William. *Hold me up, Lord.* "So your greed made you stay to wring every penny from the church. Now you're exposed, Ella." Christine's eyes darkened. Her body stiffened as she clenched and unclenched her fists.

"Now, Pastor, get the duct tape out of the drawer. I don't have time to stand around and talk to you." Ella waved the gun toward the drawer.

Christine pulled the desk drawer open and took her time searching for the roll of tape. She rattled the paper clips, pushed away the rulers, scattered the loose post-it notes throughout the drawer as she tried to devise a way to get out of the dangerous situation. *Dear Lord, I am calling on You now. Help me, please.*

She could feel her blood pulsing through her body and the adrenalin made her want to jump out of her skin. Her anger ratcheted higher as she realized how Ella manipulated her for all these months. *How could I have been so blind to her blatant deceit?*

She determined she would not allow this woman another chance to swindle and murder. She had to distract Ella, so she could get the gun away from her.

Ella continued ranting. "If William had just let it go. Him and his little rhythm band instruments. Mason had no explanation for the money missing from some insignificant music account." She mocked William's voice.

"But no, he kept checking further into more of the accounts. That night he confronted Mason about the missing money. He told him if Mason didn't go to the police, he would." Ella lowered the gun then quickly snapped it back up, keeping it leveled at Christine.

"Mason panicked. He followed William down the stairs and hit William with his cane, not just once, several times. He fell and…" With a cold, direct look at Christine, she said, "We left him there to die, to keep our secret." Ella looked down at the shaking pistol then steadied it with her other hand.

Christine steeled herself from feeling any emotion and took advantage of the moment. She flipped the roll of duct tape into the corner of the room. Ella instantly turned the gun toward the space where she heard the clatter.

At the same time, a huge vase of red roses flew through the doorway and crashed into Ella, knocking her off-balance. Before she could recover from the impact and the drenching, Lacey surged through the door and jumped on the surprised woman, pinning her to the floor. Christine dashed around the desk and picked up the gun.

"Call the police. Call the police," Lacey screamed at Christine, as she straddled Ella and forced her wrists to the floor.

Christine grabbed the phone and dialed 911.

"What is your emergency?" The nasal voice on the other end of the line grated on Christine's raw nerves.

"Hello. This is Pastor Christine Hobbs at the Dayspring Church." She took a deep breath to calm down.

"What? Dayspring Church again? Uh, go ahead."

"Yes, we need the police and an ambulance here at the church office right now." Christine looked at Ella pinned down on the floor under Lacey's petite body. "A woman was injured during a robbery."

"Where is the robber now?"

"We have her right here. The injured woman is the thief."

Chapter Twenty-Six

Cole paced the hallway of the hospital while Detective Barton sat in the family waiting lounge. It seemed they'd been there forever, anticipating the opportunity to talk with Mason. Cole pictured the old man lying on the floor of the garage with his leg twisted, he was sure the docs would have to put it together with lots of rods and wires and pins. He was no doctor. He just wanted to get in to talk to the little guy and get out of there. He wanted to see Christine after her harrowing experience at Mason's crazed hands.

He checked his watch again. Surely Ella and Christine would be coming soon. Seemed like he had been waiting on the docs and waiting for Christine forever. His patience was nearly depleted.

Thinking of Christine made him smile. Her image flashed through his mind, and he felt like a sappy sixteen-year-old kid giddy to see his girlfriend.

"Detective Stephens." A plump nurse interrupted his thoughts. "You can talk to Mr. O'Leary now." Her round face lit up. "I don't know how anxious he is to talk to you though," she said with a wink and a smile.

The detective thanked her and tapped on the

glass window of the lounge, motioning to his partner to come. He pushed open the door to Mason's room. The little man looked even smaller lying on the blue sheets in the hospital bed hooked up to an I.V. Mason's expressionless eyes followed the detectives as they approached and stood at the side of the bed.

"Hello, Mr. O'Leary. I'm Detective Stephens." Cole flashed his badge ID and ignored the one chair provided for visitors. "This is Detective Barton. He'll read you your rights."

The injured old man listened with no interruption.

"You have the right to have an attorney," Cole said.

"Why would I want an attorney? I have no defense. I'm going to jail for killing William White. Anyway, lawyers cost big money, and I'm flat broke. Ella saw to that." He lifted one hand to his forehead and raked back what few hairs he had on his bald head. "She squeezed every cent out of me. Then when she wanted more, I was dumb enough to help her steal money from my church. Of all places." He rolled his head back on his pillow and squeezed his eyes closed. "I'm sorry. I am so sorry."

Mason drew in a deep breath and flicked his gaze from one man to the other. "I guess you want to hear my story. First, however, I have some advice for you. Don't ever fall in love with a woman. I'm in all this trouble because of her." He shrugged his shoulders.

"Because of who, Mr. O'Leary?" Detective Barton waited for the answer with his notebook and pen ready to record all the information.

"It's Ella. I did it all for Ella." He lifted his hands from the bed then dropped them back to his side. "She dragged me around like a puppy dog. I loved her so much I would've given her anything. Everything. I was so dumb. I even thought she would run away with me when things got to be too, uh, complicated, but no, she didn't want me."

He turned sad eyes to the detectives. "I was such an idiot. She only wanted the money and the gifts. She didn't want me." He brushed the tears away with his fingers and wiped his nose on the back of his hand.

Then with new-found energy, he said, "I want her caught and jailed. Lock her up and throw away the key."

Cole broke out in a cold sweat. Christine was with Ella. "Excuse me." He pulled out his phone and bolted from the room. Within minutes, he returned.

"We just picked up Ella at the church. She's on her way to jail right now."

"Go ahead and tell us the whole story." Detective Barton said.

"Well, gentlemen, let me start at the beginning for you."

Cole saw the glimmer of life fill Mason's eyes as he folded his hands on his chest.

* * *

The police ushered the limping Ella out of the church and assisted the handcuffed woman into the back of the police cruiser. Christine and Lacey watched from the sidewalk.

"Wow, she's some tough gal not to have to go to the hospital after I jumped on her," Lacey said.

Christine turned to her friend and gave her a big bear hug. "Oh, Lacey, you were the instant answer to my prayer. Thank God you had a flower delivery here this afternoon!"

Lacey pulled away from the hug to face her. "You could have been killed in there! That woman was crazy." She flicked the tears away from her cheeks.

Christine patted Lacey's back as if she were soothing a child. "Are you okay? You made quite a flying leap and ended up on the floor."

"I may have a few bruises and scratches from Ella's nails. I don't need a doctor if that's what you mean."

She saw the twinkle in her friend's eyes. "So, we're all right now. I know God was watching over us and answering my prayers. God, you, me. We make a pretty good team, huh?" Christine gave her a thumbs up.

"Believe me, I was saying some prayers, too, at the moment," Lacey replied. "Give me a minute to call the shop and tell them to make up that order for the rose arrangement again, so we can deliver it in time for the anniversary celebration here tonight."

Christine gazed across the parking lot. Her heart leaped when she spied Cole pull into the parking lot and jump out of his car. Tickles of joy danced across her skin when she watched him jog across the lot toward her.

He instantly pulled her to him for a long embrace. Taking a step backward to look her over from head to toe, he asked, "You're all right? You're not hurt?"

"No, no. I'm okay. All I did was throw a roll of duct tape and make a phone call." She smiled as big as she could to convince him she truly was okay.

"Did someone interview you both? If you need to stay around, I'll wait for you." Cole crossed his arms.

"Oh, I think we're good to go. We've talked to the police. Gave them our statements. I guess that's the official way of putting it. We can go over to my house if you have time. I think Lacey and I need a minute to unwind. Okay with you, Lacey?"

"Sure. I don't need to get back to the shop. They can handle it." Turning to Cole, she said, "So where have you been? You missed all the excitement." She grinned up at the detective.

"I was at the hospital talking to Mason. He has quite the story to tell, and I'm sure you two have one also." Cole's broad smile made the day's madness melt away.

"Okay, then. I'll put on some coffee, and we can fill you in. First, I have to get an apple for Abraham. I haven't checked on him since the, uh, incident in the garage. Come on." Christine motioned for them to follow her.

The group strolled through the parking lot and across the street to the colonial house with the pig, the kangaroo, and the cat waiting for them.

* * *

The three partners-in-ending-a-crime relaxed in the spacious living room of the parsonage. Bitsy made the rounds sniffing at each one, receiving lots of petting and attention. She sauntered over to the couch and gingerly jumped up on the thick cushions. She chose her favorite place to stretch out on the back of the couch.

Christine realized the cat had found a home here with her. Bitsy had claimed her place on the couch, and Christine knew she could not bear to let her go.

The purring cat and the delicious aroma of coffee brewing in the kitchen helped to bring a sense of peace after the traumatic afternoon events.

"What exactly happened in that office today?" Cole reached for his small notepad, and then shoved it back in his pocket. Evidently he wasn't wearing his detective hat at the moment.

"Well, you know after Mason was carted off in the ambulance, I was getting ready to go to the hospital when I saw Ella was still at the church. I thought she might have fainted or something, she was so upset, so I went to check on her. The office door was locked. She didn't answer my knock on the door, so I opened it with my key and found her packing up bags. I noticed the monitor on the office computer had several church financial reports at the bottom of the screen."

She stopped to take a deep breath. She really did not want to re-live the next scenes. She stood up. "I think the coffee's done. Anybody ready for a cup yet?" Christine checked each one's face. The somber expressions didn't change.

"No, Chris, sit down. I want you to tell me while it's fresh in your mind. I realize this is difficult, but please—" His gaze wouldn't let her go. All she wanted to do was wrap her arms around his neck and hold on tight.

"Okay." She tucked a strand of hair behind her ear and sat down again on the edge of the recliner and gathered her thoughts. "I asked Ella why she was working on those files now. Instead of answering, she grabbed a gun from her purse and pointed it at me. She told me to get the roll of duct tape out of the desk drawer. I assume she wanted to tape me up, so I wouldn't call the police or chase her." Christine watched as a flash of anger washed across the detective's face. "Cole, please. I don't believe Ella would've hurt me. She was my friend as well as my secretary."

"Friends don't pull guns on friends," Lacey said. She tucked her feet up under her as she sat

170

on the ugly couch. "Just sayin'."

Christine wanted to ignore the comment, but recognized the truth in Lacey's statement. She pushed a wisp of hair behind her ear and took a deep breath before continuing her account.

"I hate to break the news to you. Ella was not the person you believe her to be," Cole said. "In fact, her name is Marie Goodman." He waited a bit for the women to absorb this revelation. "She served prison time for driving the getaway car for a boyfriend in a bank robbery about thirty years ago. She also served time for forging checks nearly fifteen years ago."

"You've got to be kidding me." Lacey's legs shot out from under her as she sat upright on the couch.

Christine's hands covered her chest." Oh, no. That's hard to believe." She sat up straight, her eyes wide in surprise. "How in the world could she have kept this information from the board? Why didn't someone find out about her background?"

"I don't know other than folks in small towns are trusting. Church members easily make friends with newcomers and include them. Once she had a circle of friends, she could have someone give her a recommendation for the secretary job. No questions asked." He shrugged his shoulders. "I don't know how she got the job. That will definitely be at the top of our investigation...to see who else is involved with the scheme."

Lacey and Christine exchanged looks. Christine couldn't imagine a ring of thieves in the church spreading like a virus.

"When I confronted her, she told me William found out about the missing money cover-up. She admitted she and Mason were doing it. She never mentioned anyone else." Christine eyed Cole for a reaction, but he didn't reveal any emotion.

Cole turned to Lacey. "So when did you get involved in all of this, Lacey?"

Lacey wrinkled her nose. "I came in the church to deliver a vase of roses for an anniversary party tonight." She glanced at Christine.

"As I walked down the hall, I heard Ella and Chris talking. I was going to stop in and say hi. Then I heard Ella order Chris to get the duct tape out of the drawer. And it wasn't in a friendly tone. As I got closer, Ella said Mason hit William with a cane. That's when I rushed to the door and just threw what I had in my hands at her. Unfortunately, it was a hundred dollars worth of roses." Rolling her eyes, Lacey puckered up her lips and blew out a shrill whistle.

"The roses startled Ella, and she dropped the gun. I rushed her, knocked her down, and Christine grabbed the gun and called the police." Lacey sat back on the couch to catch her breath.

"I can't believe Mason killed William. I

think she was lying," Christine said.

"Believe it. Mason confessed this afternoon. He implicated Ella saying it was her idea to embezzle from the church treasury. Unfortunately, William figured it out. Mason didn't want Ella to have to go to jail again if William went to the police. So on an impulse, he followed William down the steps to the basement. When he got behind him, he whacked him with that silver-knobbed cane. We found it in his car. The lab is checking it for evidence. William fell with such force he broke his neck. He was dead when he landed on the floor at the bottom of the stairs."

Christine sucked in her breath and squeezed her eyes closed to block out the image in her memory. Lacey covered her mouth and lowered her gaze to the floor. Silence blanketed the room like a thick storm cloud.

Christine looked at Cole. He said nothing, but his loving gaze comforted her. She was thankful he was giving them a chance to absorb all the emotions that came with this explosive information.

"Why? Why would they steal from the church?" Lacey opened her hands toward Cole seeking an answer.

"Mason loved her. He was head over heels in love with her. Think about it. This little guy never got noticed by the ladies. So when Ella showed an interest in him, he gave her everything he could to keep her, except she wanted more. So to finance the jewelry and clothes for her, he helped her steal the money."

"What a fool. Blinded by love, huh?" Lacey shook her head.

"I guess I was a fool, too. Ella certainly had me convinced she was a good, kind woman. My friend as well as secretary. She betrayed me." Christine's voice broke with emotion.

Lacey and Cole moved to Christine. She stood to embrace them. Standing in the middle of the living room, they held the group hug for several moments, gathering strength and comfort from each other.

Chapter Twenty-Seven

"All right, I better get over to the hospital to see Mason." Christine placed her empty cup by the sink.

"Chris." Cole set his cup on the counter and turned her around. "Are you sure you want to talk to Mason?"

"Yes, I do. I'm his pastor. He needs God more than ever, and I'm God's messenger."

"And Ella?"

She placed her hands gently on Cole's shoulders as he slipped his arms around her waist. "Yes, if she wants to talk to me, I think we both have things to take to God together."

"Well, how can I argue with that? You're right." Cole pecked her cheek and gave her a quick hug. "I'll see you tonight." He winked and gave her the smile that melted her heart.

"See you later, Lacey," he said as she walked into the kitchen.

"Hmmmm…" Lacey watched the good-looking detective leave through the kitchen door. "What just happened here?"

"What?" She flashed a grin at Lacey. "Do you mean that little kiss and a hug from Cole? Or do you mean the crazy afternoon of interrogation by the detective?" Christine rinsed the cups and set them in the drainer.

"You know what I mean. That guy wants you. How do you feel about him? Is the feeling mutual?" Lacey arched an eyebrow.

"Well, you certainly are full of questions." Christine chuckled. "Honestly? I think we're sliding into love. I wasn't looking for it. In fact, I'm a bit afraid to go there again."

Christine grabbed the towel off the counter and wiped her hands. She gazed intently at her friend. "I don't know if I can trust my feelings about people anymore. I loved Brad and look what happened. And now with Ella. I thought she was a friend, but she manipulated me as well as Mason. I was completely blindsided by her."

Lacey reached for Christine's hands and held them tightly. "Oh, how I wish I could tell you everything is going to be all right. I wish I knew the future. I just know if you're too afraid to take a risk, you may regret it the rest of your life. What's that old saying? It's better to have loved and lost, than never to have loved at all."

"Sure. It's easy to say that. Right now, my heart wants to believe it, however my brain does *not* agree with the statement." She squeezed Lacey's hands. *Thank You, Lord, for this beloved friend.*

* * *

Pastor Christine sat alone in the back pew of the quiet sanctuary. Only the moonlight through the long wall of windows in the room illuminated the large space. Thoughts of this day filled with terror and discovery tumbled around in her mind.

The time with Mason in the hospital was fresh in her memory. He had been groggy from the leg surgery, although he was aware enough to say he was so sorry for what he had done.

"I'm a foolish old man, Pastor. I thought Ella loved me. I didn't want to lose her." He brushed away a tear from his eye with the back of his hand.

"She was the light of my life, the center of my world. I cannot believe she used me like that...or that I could be manipulated so easily. I thought I was a smart guy. I guess not when it comes to love." He picked up his handkerchief and blew so hard into it Christine thought every person on the floor of the hospital heard him.

"I know I can't make excuses for my actions. Ella didn't hold a gun to my head to make me do it."

Christine shuddered at the memory of Ella aiming the gun at her.

"I don't think God will ever forgive me for stealing from the church and killing William. I'm a thief and a murderer. I can't forgive myself," he said. He shook his head as the tears coursed down his cheeks.

She pulled a tissue from the box and gave it to the guilt-ridden man. "God is with you right now, Mason. Don't you remember in Romans it says nothing will ever separate you from God's love? God is here crying right along with you and will never leave you." She reached for his hand. *"You'll have to face the truth and take your punishment, but God will be standing beside you to give you strength to handle the ordeal. You have to ask for forgiveness and mean it."* She held his hand to impart comfort and support.

"Will you allow me to pray now for God's grace to strengthen you and help find the peace and the forgiveness you need to face what is ahead of you?"

Mason nodded in agreement to the prayer then clung to her hand as if hanging on to a life-saving rope.

* * *

In the quiet sanctuary, she squeezed her eyes shut, trying to erase the thoughts invading her own prayers. She wanted to remember the happier times with memories of William and the sound of his laughter throughout the church, Mason and his leprechaun tricks and fun, Ella laughing with her about the cat, Ella helping her unpack and settle in to her new home and church.

However, it wasn't easy to block the heart-wrenching events so clearly etched into her memory. The crazed look on Mason's face as he aimed the rifle at her, Ella and her cold, heartless confession. Her face burned with the realization of how easily Ella had wormed her way into her heart. Seeing into Ella's hate-filled eyes as she told her how she had used Mason was the defining moment she'd realized how evil and conniving Ella was. Christine tried to blink away the scenes, put them in a far corner of her mind, but they continued to play on a loop inside her head.

Finally, the image of Cole blotted out all the darkness of the day's events. She couldn't help but smile when she pictured him pulling Abraham off Mason, waiting by the bathroom door to be sure she was okay after the ordeal with Mason, and listening with concern to Lacey's story. The warmth she felt in his arms was something she would treasure forever, along with his kisses, so sweet and full of tenderness. She wet her lips, wishing he were here with her now.

As she sat with bowed head, Christine hummed the song that always centered her for prayer, "You are My All in All:"

"You are my strength when I am weak. You are the treasure that I seek. You are my all in all."

Christine felt God's love and peace envelop her. *Dear God of love and power, You are so awesome. Let my lips praise You and thank You for my many blessings. I come to You this evening with a heavy heart. I confess I have not handled the situations as well as I should have. I pray You'll forgive me for my selfishness and feelings of hate. Help me to be open to You, to listen, to love.* She had so much to bring to God.

First on her mind was Mason. He hated himself for what he had done.

She scooted to the edge of the cushioned pew and sat up straight, her fingers woven together in an attitude for prayer. *Lord, please hold Mason in Your heart tonight and forgive him for his sins. He lost his way; please help him find the path to Your grace and peace.*

Christine shook her head because she knew she needed to do some work in the forgiving arena in her own life. She wanted to forgive her ex-husband, Brad, and her secretary, Ella, for betrayals against her. She wilted a bit in her seat then sat tall again. *Speaking of forgiveness, Lord, I know I need to forgive Brad for his betrayal and breaking my heart.* Sitting in the stillness of the sanctuary, she allowed herself a moment to absorb this idea completely and to wash away the bitterness and pain of Brad's treachery. *Please help me to let that hurt go, so I can be open to experience love again. He has established his new life, and I am experiencing a new life here that I love. Thank You for the opportunity to serve You at this church and for the new friends I have who are supporting me.* She frowned when she thought of her false friend, Ella.

You know I am raw and hurting after learning how Ella deceived me. I feel like an idiot for not recognizing her so-called friendship for what it was, an opportunity to steal from my beloved congregation. I need You to help me begin the road to forgiveness for her heinous crimes. A sob caught in her throat. She took a deep breath and continued. *I pray You'll work through me to help her find your grace and forgiveness.*

She rested her hands on the back of the pew ahead of her and scanned the front of the sanctuary. Her eyes rested on the large wooden cross, affixed to the wall above the altar. Spotlighted by a shaft of moonlight, the cross seemed to glow. She couldn't help but grin. *God is listening and sending me a sign of his loving kindness with this dazzling display in front of me.*

Filled with the comfort from above, she felt the assurance of support from God. With counseling and prayer, she knew she and the caring "saints" in her church could work together to support the church family through all the trials ahead.

Again she sat up straight and folded her hands to concentrate on her prayers. *Dearest Lord, I am asking for guidance and wisdom to bring love and understanding to our church members.* She knew they expected justice for the murder of their beloved music director; however, she did not want them to wish for revenge. *Help us to work together to move on and become stronger and enthusiastic witnesses for You.*

I ask You, Dear God, for strength and courage for me to face these next difficult days. The hurdles seem so high to clear, and I know You will be there with us to hold us up. She raised her hands toward Heaven.

Thank You, Lord, for loving me, for Your loving-kindness.

She breathed deeply, feeling the joy of emptying her soul to God. She relaxed and immediately her thoughts drifted to Cole. She replayed the image of his loving eyes and the feel of his gentle touch on her skin. Her heart beat rapidly, remembering his powerful embrace as he held her close in his arms.

Christine's eyes misted over as she bowed her head. *Dear God, I'm no expert when it comes to love. I bungled it with Brad. I thought I didn't want to give my heart to another man. But somehow I listened and followed Your directions to find Cole. Thank You. I don't want to ruin our relationship. I'm going to need lots of help to keep me straight and focused to navigate the path of love. I believe I can trust him with my heart.* She sucked in her breath. *I love him, Lord.* There she finally admitted it. Would he love her in return?

With an open heart she added, *I promise I'll listen and pay attention to any and all signs and messages sent from Heaven.* And with that she gave up her anxiety about Cole. The layers of grief, sadness, and doubts fell away from her like a heavy cape sliding off her shoulders. It was all in God's hands now. Releasing a deep breath, she sat back in the pew, completely drained.

Thank You for watching over me today and every day. I know You're with me always. In

Jesus' name, I pray, Amen

When she stood up from the pew, she saw Cole standing in the doorway of the sanctuary. She held on to the back of the pew to steady herself and lifted her other hand to her chest to calm her dancing heart. He was there. He was waiting for her.

Crossing through the shafts of moonbeams lighting her way to him, she felt weightless and full of joy. When they met in the doorway, Cole wrapped her in his arms. She nestled into him luxuriating in the warmth of his embrace. Her body tingled with desire.

He stepped an arm's length away from her and looked her up and down. Cole furrowed his brow when he spoke. "I was so worried about you." He motioned to the pew against the back wall. "Let's sit over there." He escorted her to the seat where they sat close together holding hands.

"I was worried about you because I know how devoted you were to Ella." He hesitated then pulled her to him cradling her in his arms. "Discovering she and Mason were the ones responsible for William's death is a lot to handle." He touched her face.

"In this moonlight, I can see you're actually smiling. You must have found peace with the situation. I should've known. You're an amazing person." He gave her a quick hug, and then sat back still gazing into her eyes.

"You don't need to worry about me. I'm much stronger now and ready to face the next steps in putting this case to rest, so we can move on from here. I'm so happy you're here, Cole." She couldn't stop looking at him.

"I told you I'd be back tonight, didn't I?" He flashed that smile that made her feel a bit light-headed.

"Yes, you did." She brushed her lips across his. "I've been thinking about you all day."

"Hey, that's funny. I've been thinking about you all day."

"Oh, really? Well, tell me what you were thinking, and then I'll tell you what I was thinking." She unfolded from his arms, her eyes sparkling with anticipation.

"Well," he looked up to the church rafters and then into her eyes. He shifted in his seat. "I finally figured out I couldn't stop thinking about you because..." He cleared his throat. "I love you."

Christine tried to keep her heart from dancing out of her chest. "Oh, Cole, that's exactly what I was thinking about today! I love you, too." She threw her arms around him. Their lips met to seal their confessions of love with a deep kiss.

She snuggled deeper into his hold, breathed the scent of him, and relaxed in his embrace. She knew this was the place to be, right here, right now, in the arms of the one she loved. Her heart filled to overflowing when she gave away a part of her heart and received his in return.

Lifting her head from his shoulder, Christine turned her face to Heaven and winked.

She smiled and sent a silent prayer,
 Now this is one large, flashing neon sign
from Heaven. Thank You, God.
 Amen, she thought, *so be it.*

The End

IF YOU ENJOYED THIS BOOK, PLEASE LEAVE A REVIEW.

J.Q. Rose from Books We Love

Deadly Undertaking
Terror on Sunshine Boulevard

J Q Rose is an avid reader, photographer, and blogger with blogs about the writing process and growing a vegetable garden. Janet and her husband are snowbirds who spend winters in Florida allowing them to garden twelve months out of the year. Summer finds her up north camping and hunting toads, frogs, and salamanders with her grandchildren.

Connect online with J.Q. Rose at:

J.Q. Rose blog http://www.jqrose.com/

Facebook http://facebook.com/jqroseauthor